D1096651

the

disappearing

boy

Praise for Sonia Tilson

Shortlisted, 2010-2011 Metcalf-Rooke Award
Finalist, 2014 Ottawa Book Awards

"There is a whole body of literature concerned with the empathy gap between parents and their grown-up children...Ottawa's Sonia Tilson has mined this emotional material for an engrossing and ambitious debut novel."

–**Zoe Whittall**, 2016 Giller Prize shortlisted author of *The Best Kind of People* for *The National Post,* on *The Monkey Puzzle Tree*

"Tilson's engaging story features a host of memorable minor characters on both sides of the Atlantic, and it culminates in a most satisfying confront-the-abuser scene. A fine first novel."

–**Cynthia Flood**, Journey Prize-winning author of *Red Girl Rat Boy,* on *The Monkey Puzzle Tree*

the

disappearing

boy

SONIA TILSON

NIMBUS
PUBLISHING

Copyright © 2017, Sonia Tilson

All rights reserved. No part of this book may be reproduced, stored in a retrieval system or transmitted in any form or by any means without the prior written permission from the publisher, or, in the case of photocopying or other reprographic copying, permission from Access Copyright, 1 Yonge Street, Suite 1900, Toronto, Ontario M5E 1E5.

Nimbus Publishing Limited
3731 Mackintosh St, Halifax, NS B3K 5A5
(902) 455-4286 nimbus.ca

Printed and bound in Canada

NB1287

This novel is a work of fiction. Names, characters, places, and incidents are either the product of the author's imagination or are used fictitiously.

Design: Jenn Embree

Library and Archives Canada Cataloguing in Publication

Tilson, Sonia, author
The disappearing boy / Sonia Tilson.
Issued in print and electronic formats.
ISBN 978-1-77108-548-9 (softcover).--ISBN 978-1-77108-549-6
(HTML)
    I. Title.

PS8639.I557D57 2017   jC813'.6   C2017-904119-3
C2017-904120-7

Nimbus Publishing acknowledges the financial support for its publishing activities from the Government of Canada, the Canada Council for the Arts, and from the Province of Nova Scotia. We are pleased to work in partnership with the Province of Nova Scotia to develop and promote our creative industries for the benefit of all Nova Scotians.

chapter 1

*T*URNING THE CORNER TO HIS NEW
house, Neil shivered and heaved up his backpack. Ottawa was a lot colder than Vancouver.
Not so long ago, he'd been skateboarding with
his friends in the sunshine at Stanley Park. Here,
although it was only October, a cold wind seemed
to be blowing all the time. People hurried along,
heads down, clutching their briefcases, listening
to their headphones. Even the dogs looked like
they just wanted to get home.

He stopped at the townhouse and stared up at the red-brick front of his new home. It was okay, he supposed. It was one in an identical row of six, bigger and grander than the little bungalow they'd left behind in Vancouver. His bedroom here was bigger too, with room for bookshelves and a work table and an armchair. There was even room on the top floor for his mom to have a studio. It had a pathetic little yard though, and no view worth talking about. He wondered if this house would ever feel like home.

He opened the gate and fished around in his pocket for his key, then unlocked the front door and pushed his way inside.

"Hi, sweetie." He heard his mother first, before she came out of the kitchen into the hallway. She was wearing a red-striped apron over her soft wool sweater and long swishy skirt.

"You're home," he said, surprised.

She smiled, tossing her dark hair behind her shoulders. "I had the afternoon off." She helped him with his coat, reaching around to hang it in the closet as he shucked off his shoes. "How was school?"

"It was okay," he said. He wanted to tell her about the painting he'd done in art class. It was of the view from the old bungalow's front window, with yachts in the bay and the sun on the mountains. He'd kind of liked it, but it wasn't real art, not like his mom's work. He decided to keep it to himself. "We started a new book in English," he told her instead, *"A Wrinkle in Time."*

"I've read it," she said. "It's wonderful! One of those books you never forget."

"Cool. So...how was your day?" His mom had only just started her new job at the children's hospital, where she helped sick kids have some fun and maybe express their feelings through drawing and painting and making stuff. "I bet the kids really liked messing around with paints."

"It was great," she said, but then looked away, her smile fading. "But there's this little boy, Jeremy, who has pretty serious cancer. He drew a picture of himself flying to the moon in his pajamas." She shook her head. "He's only six."

"Oh." Neil let the image sink in. "But he'll be all right, won't he? He'll get better?"

"I don't know, Neil. But I do know he was happy for a while today, poor little guy." She went into the kitchen. "Why don't you wash up and then come help me? I knew you'd be hungry, so I'm making dinner a bit early. We're having haddock, and French fries from scratch."

Neil enjoyed cooking with his mother. As she set about breading the fish for the oven, he dragged the familiar beat-up wooden cutting board from its home beside the microwave.

He chopped tomatoes for a salad, and listened to his mother humming as she moved about the kitchen. It actually felt like a bit like home for the first time since they'd moved in.

When dinner was ready, they took their places at either end of the table and settled down to enjoy the meal. The fish was tender and crispy and the fries were perfect.

The fish scraps made Neil think of his little cat, which they'd left behind in Vancouver. He looked sideways at his mother. "Perkins would have loved this," he said, as he scraped bits of fish skin to the side of his plate.

She closed her eyes. "Oh, not that again, sweetie." She stood up. "I know you miss Perkins, Neil, but bringing him here would have been just too difficult. Remember, we had no idea where we were going to live, and Perkins would have been traumatized by the flight." She reached across the table to pick up his plate. "Anyway, you know he'll be happy with the Thompsons. He spent half his time around there when you were at school, and they positively begged to have him. He loved them, Neil. I'm sure he's happy there."

She took the dirty dishes into the kitchen and Neil got up from his chair and followed her.

"But he loved us more," he said as she put the dishes into the dishwasher. He felt tears pricking his eyes. "Remember how he used to follow me down the street, meowing, and cuddle up to me at night, purring his head off? He misses me, I know he does."

Neil's mom took a deep breath. He could tell she was frustrated. "I'm sorry Neil, but what's done is done. We had enough on our plate without figuring out how to deal with Perkins, and that's all I'm going to say on the matter."

"Why did we have to come here anyway?" he said, his voice raised. "You never asked me if I wanted to move. You never tell me anything. You treat me like a little kid!"

"Oh Neil, that's not true. I know the move was hard on you, but I had my reasons for coming here. Believe it or not, it's not easy being a single parent. It's hard always making these decisions by myself."

"You say you're always by yourself. Why is that anyway? Why are you by yourself?" Fixing his eyes on hers, he said quietly, "What happened to my father?"

After a long pause, she sighed heavily. "I don't know what's happening to us, Neil," she said, her shoulders slumping. "We used to get along so well, didn't we? But you've changed so much lately. You're so quick to get angry with me." She put her hand on his arm. "I do understand that there are things you want to know, and I *will* tell them to you," she said. "Not right now, but very soon. I promise."

He pulled his arm away. "Soon. That's what you always say. Why not now?" He stared hard at her. "Is he dead?"

She looked away, sighing, but didn't answer him.

"If he is dead, how did he die? Did he get sick? Was he in an accident?" He took a sharp breath. "Was he murdered?"

"For heaven's sake, Neil! Of course not. Don't be so melodramatic." She turned away, but Neil wasn't finished yet. He needed to know. He was sick of her pushing aside his questions.

"Did he kill himself?" he said. "Or did he murder someone and get put into prison for life?" His mother left the kitchen, but he persisted, following her into the living room. "If it wasn't any of those things, and he just ran off and left us," he said to her rigid back, "what's the big deal? Lots of dads do that."

"Stop it Neil!" She put up a hand to shush him, but he wasn't done. The questions had been piling up in his mind for too long. He needed answers.

"Is he in a hospital somewhere? Or locked up in an insane asylum? Or"—this was his latest theory—"is he a spy, involved in top-secret missions that we're not allowed to know about?" He realized he was shouting, but he didn't care. "Don't I have a right to know?"

"It's complicated, Neil," she said firmly. "But I promise I *will* tell you all about it when the time is right, which will be very soon." She sat on the sofa and patted the cushion beside her. "Come and sit by me for a minute, sweetie."

He stood looking down at her, his arms folded.

"Suit yourself," she said. "But there's something I want you to do for me, Neil. I think it will make a big difference to both of us."

"What is it?" he asked, interested despite himself.

She looked up at him, her eyes wide and anxious. "There's someone I want you to meet."

"Who?"

"My mother."

"Your mother?" he repeated, trying to understand.

"Yes," she said. "Your grandmother."

"What do you mean?" he asked, his voice barely a squeak. "I have a grandmother? Here? In Ottawa?"

"Yes."

"And you didn't tell me?" He sat on the edge of the sofa, shocked. This was the first he'd heard of any grandmother. "Have you been to see her?"

"Yes, I have. I wanted to go alone the first time.... We haven't spoken for several years."

"Why not?" he demanded. "Does it have something to do with my father?"

She sighed. "Yes, in a way it does. But I'm hoping that you and I can begin to spend time with her now that we live here. I'd really like for you to meet her, Neil, and I know that she'd love to meet you."

He considered this. "When do you want us to go see her?"

His mother reached out and put a hand on his knee. "Actually, Neil, she and I have agreed that you should visit her by yourself at first. You could get to know each other better that way than if I were with you. I know it seems odd, but I promise, everything will make sense in time."

"In time...in time...." He pushed her hand off and jumped up, frustrated. "Why do you always keep me waiting like this, Mom?"

"But will you go, Neil?"

He sat down again. "Whatever. Guess I don't have much choice."

chapter 2

NEIL SLOUCHED ACROSS THE PARK, kicking a pebble through the wet, yellow leaves. He was still brooding over the fact that he was nearly fourteen and didn't know a thing about his own father. Now his mother had dropped a brand-new mystery into his lap: Margaret MacLeod, his grandmother—a grandmother he'd never even known about. It was all so weird. He booted the pebble into the gutter and checked his phone.

This was Mercier Street, all right, and there was the house, facing him from across the road. He could see the numbers beside the door: a six and an eight in dull gold against the dark brick wall.

Like the other houses on the block, this one was half of a pair, their second floors joined over a shared driveway. The dried-up roses hanging their heads in number sixty-eight's little front yard didn't look at all inviting. Neither did the lacy, old-lady drapes. He shoved his phone into his pocket, wishing he hadn't agreed to come.

As he stepped onto the small walkway in front of the house, he turned to see a girl charging down the sidewalk towards him. A long black coat flapped behind her and as she got closer, he noticed a stud gleaming from her lower lip.

To Neil's surprise, she stopped when she reached him. Up close, he realized that, despite the coat and piercing, she was around his age, probably no more than fourteen. Eyebrows raised, she looked him up and down with a crooked little smile.

"You visiting Margaret?" she said.

"Uh-huh."

"You a friend of hers?"

It was none of her business, but Neil didn't want to offend her. "She's my grandmother."

The girl did a double take. "No way! I've lived next door to Margaret for years and she never said she had any family. Are you from away, or what?"

"Yeah. From Vancouver. We just moved here a few weeks ago."

"Huh! Whad'ya know?" She tilted her head, considering. "My name's Courtenay."

"Hi. I'm Neil."

"Cool. See you around, Neil." As fast as she'd appeared, she moved up the walk and unlocked the door of number seventy. She turned, giving him a big grin, and then pushed inside the door, banging it shut behind her.

Neil pulled the hood tighter around his face, and walked up to the door of number sixty-eight. He waited for a minute, then poked the doorbell. Nobody answered. He shuffled on and off the step a few times, his laces trailing in a puddle, and then put an ear to the glass and squinted through the lace curtain. There was no sound or movement. Blowing his hair off his nose in a mixture of disappointment and relief, he turned, and was about to leave, when the door creaked open behind him.

"Neil?"

Ducking his head, he turned to squint at the tall, thin old woman in the doorway. She smiled and opened the door wider.

"Please come in," she said. "I'm so glad you came!" She stood back. "My goodness, you're tall for your age," she said as he edged past her. "Now, turn around and let me look at you." She stepped in behind him and closed the door.

He shucked off his wet Nikes and turned to glance shyly at her through his lashes.

"Oh! Right." Her voice had gotten strange, Neil noticed, shakier and a bit rough.

"Come on in." She pointed to a high-backed armchair in the living room. "Make yourself comfortable and I'll get you a bite to eat."

Settling himself in the chair, he looked around the room. This was the smallest house he'd ever been in, but it was cozy. The colours were soft and warm, the old-fashioned furniture shone, and the winged armchair was really comfy. Tired after the long walk, he stretched out his feet and leaned his head back. Gentle clinks came from the kitchen, along with the smell of something delicious.

His eyes stopped at a painting beside a small window. He stood up and walked over to the wall to get a better look. The thick sweeps of scarlet, green, and deep blue, edged by black slashes and lit by jagged streaks of lemon, reminded him of his mother's paintings, but this was much rougher and wilder—savage even. His art teacher in Vancouver would have called it abstract, but it didn't feel abstract to him. It felt real, like someone was suddenly in the room with him.

He got back to the chair just as his grandmother came in carrying a tray.

"There you go." She put the tray down on the little table beside him. His mouth watered at the sight of freshly baked cookies, along with a tall glass of milk. "I made these especially for you," she said. "Dig in."

Neil realized he was starving and got started on the cookies. They were delicious, the chocolate chips still half melted. He washed them down with gulps of cold milk, and then smiled at his grandmother.

"They're good," he said. "Thanks."

She smiled back at him. "Did your mother tell you who I am, Neil?" she asked.

He nodded, suddenly awkward, then grabbed another cookie and fixed his eyes on the carpet; chewing carefully, he focused on its complicated pattern of dark red, navy blue, and gold.

"What exactly did she say?" she asked.

He swallowed. "She said, um, she said you're her mother...my grandmother?" He looked up at her.

"That's right. I'm Sasha's mother." She smiled. Looking at her properly for the first time, he could see the likeness to his mom in the slightly curved nose and brown, downward-sloping eyes, and in the thick dark hair springing back from a point in the middle of her forehead.

"You don't have to call me Grandma, of course," she said. "Call me Margaret if you like." She smiled again. "I hope we can become friends."

Was she serious? She seemed nice enough, but she was old, with gray hair and wrinkles. He wondered again why his mother had never mentioned her before.

She walked to a cabinet in the corner, opened a drawer, and pulled something out, glancing at it briefly before handing it to him. "Here. Your mother says you like horses."

It was an old photograph, Neil realized, taking it from her. He examined it carefully and saw a smiling man leaning against a dark horse, its head bent towards him, the arched neck and long, surprisingly light-coloured mane making it look like a knight's charger. He dreamed of being able to ride a horse someday. Maybe, if he ever got rich enough, he would even have one of his own.

"Who is this?" he asked.

"That's your grandfather, Ken," she said. "And that's Dude, his prized Rocky Mountain horse." She paused. "You look a bit like Ken, you know. You have his eyes."

"My grandfather," he repeated. This was a lot to absorb in one day.

He studied the man. He was small and square, with fairish hair, sticking-out ears, and a big grin. "Where does he live?" he asked.

"Near Saint John, New Brunswick," she said.

"Does he still have horses?" he asked.

"Yes," she said, gently taking the photo and replacing it in the drawer. "He has a small stable, I believe."

Neil's eyes went back to the painting.

His grandmother's gaze followed his and she smiled. She walked over to where it hung on the wall. "You like this, do you?" She touched the frame, staring at the painting for a moment, then turned back to him. "Your father was very proud of this one."

Neil stared at her. *What did she just say?* He felt the house shake as a car rumbled past the side wall. "Did you say my father painted that?"

His grandmother's smile disappeared. A robin crash-landed on a bush outside the window, flying off again at the slam of a car door. She turned to the window to watch the bird's flight.

"Yes," she said finally, her voice distant. "He painted it when he was nineteen and studying art at university." She turned back to him. "He won a prize for it."

Neil went over to study the painting again. It looked like a struggle between light and darkness, rise and fall, shapes and spaces, with everything pushing and pulling and yet somehow belonging together. There was a name scrawled at the bottom right: *Adam.* He turned to her, his mouth dry. "You know my father?"

She looked trapped, her eyes shifting the way his mother's had when he'd confronted her the other day.

"I do," she said. "I mean, I did." A siren wailed down the street. She caught her breath. "I mean...."

"You did? What do you mean, you did?" His voice cracked and then boomed: "Is my father dead?"

He was trying hard not to cry. "Tell me! You've got to tell me what happened to him. What happened to my father?"

"I'm sorry, Neil, I can't tell you that," she said abruptly. "But I can tell you that he's not dead." She paused, and turned away from his angry face. "Your mother must tell you the rest."

Unbelievable. He clenched his fists, the nails digging into his palms. *Here we go again.*

She cleared her throat. "Please Neil, don't be angry. Your mother loves you very much. And so do I." She carefully lifted the painting off the wall. "You can have this if you want," she said. "I always meant it for you."

His eyes jumped from her to the painting, the hairs on the back of his neck prickling. This scary creation, dreamed up and slashed onto the canvas by his father, this could belong to him for real? Maybe it could tell him who his father really was, or at least what it was like to be him. Maybe it could lead him to his father. He straightened his back, composing himself.

"Well, what do you think?" she asked. "Would you like to have it, Neil?"

"Yes," he said, his heart bumping in his throat. "Please."

Their eyes stayed on the painting as Margaret handed it to Neil. This wasn't his father, Neil thought, but for now, it was the closest he'd ever come to finding him.

chapter 3

NEIL SPRAWLED ON HIS BED AND studied the details of the painting, trying to figure out what made it so powerful. He couldn't wait to visit again next Sunday to see what else he might find out. Maybe he'd get to see that girl again too, Courtenay.

With a funny feeling in his stomach, he remembered the way the girl had turned and smiled at him from her front door. He'd never had a girlfriend, but she'd seemed kind of approachable—and more real somehow than most of the girls he'd met. Maybe she could be a friend anyway.

Neil lay back, his hands behind his head, thinking about his visit. So, now he had a nice, kind grandmother, Margaret. And it seemed he also had a faraway grandfather, Ken. Ken had looked kind of friendly and cheerful in the photo, Neil thought. He wondered if he would ever get to meet him.

He sat up and looked around the room. The best place for the painting, he decided, would be across from his bed, where he would see it as soon as he woke up. He got up and examined the wall, then grabbed a pencil from his desk and drew an X. In the basement, he dug around in the unpacked boxes until he managed to find his mother's tool-box, and dragged out a hammer and a nail.

He climbed on a chair to get a better angle and placed the point of the big black nail on the centre of the X. He gripped the hammer half-way up the handle and gave the nail a firm tap. Nothing happened. He shifted his grip and hammered harder until a good whack finally drove the point of the nail into the wall, but when he took his fingers away the nail fell to the ground.

He got the point back in and gave the nail several more whacks. This seemed to work, although some cracks appeared in the wall along with a shower of plaster. Finally, he succeeded in driving the nail in.

His mom wasn't going to like the mess on the floor, he thought, never mind the cracks, but that was just too bad. Anyway, the painting would probably cover most of the damage.

He raised the hammer for one last bash at the nail when he heard the front door open. Someone ran up the stairs and his bedroom door opened. His mother stood in the doorway.

"What's going on, Neil?" she asked. "I could hear the hammering from the street." She looked past him at the wall. "Look what you've done! You've just about ruined that wall." She sighed. "What were you thinking, Neil? There are special nails, you know, for hanging pictures, so that this sort of thing doesn't happen."

Red-faced and sweaty, Neil climbed down from the chair. He was above his mother's shoulder in height now, he saw, as they stood face to face, and people said he still had a lot of growing to do. "I wanted to hang something," he said defiantly.

Her gaze shifted to the painting propped against the wall, its back towards her. "What is that, anyway? What's so important that it couldn't wait until I came home?"

"I wanted to get it up now," he said. "And I didn't see why I should have to wait until you decided to come home." He walked past her towards the door. "What's for dinner?"

She took off her raincoat. "We're having one of your favourites tonight," she said. "Sausage, mashed potatoes and peas, and blueberry pie." She smiled. "Aren't you going to ask me about my day?"

"Oh, yeah. Right. How was it?" Anxious to get her away from the painting, Neil jerked his head at the door. "Let's go. I'm hungry."

"Wait a minute, Neil," she said. "I want to hear all about your visit with Margaret. I've been thinking about it all afternoon." She glanced down at the picture. "But first, let's have a look at this." She bent to pick it up.

"No!" He pushed past her and snatched the painting from her before she could turn it around. Clutching it to his chest, he glared at her. "My grandmother gave me this. She said she always meant for me to have it. She said my father painted it!"

He lifted his chin and said, "I'm putting it up on my wall, Mom, and there's nothing you can do about it."

He got back up on the chair with it and glared down at her over his shoulder. "Even if you don't want anything of his around here, you're not taking this away from me." He arranged the painting until it hung straight. "It's mine. You got that?"

There was no answer. He stepped down from the chair and saw that his mother had slumped onto the bed and was staring, bug-eyed, at the painting. She'd obviously seen it before, in Margaret's house, so why was she was gawking at it now? Why did she look so shocked?

Neil went to the far end of the room to see for himself. The painting was even more stunning in its new home. It blazed out of the surrounding whiteness: "*I am here!*" it seemed to shout, "*Look at me!*" and even, he imagined, "*Set me free!*"

His mother, white-faced, was holding out her hand. "Neil, sweetheart, we need to talk—"

He turned on her. "I'm sick of you and your so-called talks. You never tell me anything. You keep putting me off and putting me off until I can't stand it anymore. I'm out of here." He looked back at the painting. "And you know what?

I'm taking this with me, because I don't trust you with it." He yanked the painting off the nail and strode out of the room.

"Wait, Neil!" He heard her call as he ran off. "I need to tell you something."

He didn't care. He just needed to get away.

He shoved his feet down into his boots, and tugged his coat on. Then he shot through the door, slamming it shut behind him.

chapter 4

THE RIDEAU CENTRE WAS A BIG downtown mall, as busy and noisy as the ones in Vancouver and just as cool as the kids at school had said, except that Neil didn't know anyone here. Still, there was lots of stuff to look at and at least he and the painting were inside, away from the threat of rain.

Neil wondered what he'd been thinking, dragging a painting across town. He stopped and looked down at it. It was big and awkward.

Maybe he could find a big enough bag to carry it around in. He took the escalator up to the Dollar Store on the third floor, where the only thing he could find big enough was a glossy bag in a gross shade of green.

He stopped outside a gallery store and peered at the paintings that hung in the window. He considered them carefully, then peeked inside the bag at his father's painting. You only had to give that other stuff half a look to see how good an artist his father was. When Neil found his father, he'd show him the portfolio he'd already started to put together at his new art teacher's suggestion. He might like some of it. Perhaps his father could teach him and they could even work together. Maybe.

He sat on the slatted wooden bench and checked his watch. It was already ten past six, and he was hungry. He'd better get a hamburger and fries at the food court. He had enough money for that, and the mall was open late since it was Friday, so he was okay for a few hours. But then what? He hung his head, staring down between his knees at the empty drink carton and bent plastic straw at his feet. Under the edge of the bench his fingers met a rock-hard wad of gum. He rubbed his hands on his jeans. No way was he going home. It was time his mother learned he wasn't going to be silenced anymore.

The problem was, he didn't have anywhere else to go in Ottawa. He knew his grandmother would just call his mom right away, so that was no good. He couldn't crash at a friend's house, because he didn't really have any friends. Not yet, at least, although there were some possibilities shaping up. There was Hiu, for instance, the guy he'd been paired up with in French. Hiu seemed really cool, and he even had family in Vancouver, but they didn't really know each other yet.

And then there was Courtenay, the girl he'd met on his grandmother's street. She'd seemed friendly. He wondered if she went to his school, and imagined bumping into her by the lockers at the end of the school day. She might recognize him and smile that funny smile, and suggest they walk some of the way home together. He shook his head and stood up.

In the food court, he poked at the pale, limp fries with a white plastic fork and shoved aside the gray, uneaten hamburger. He remembered the dinner his mom had planned: fat brown sausages, creamy potatoes, and blueberry pie topped with plain vanilla ice cream, the way he liked it.

He took a gulp of Coke. The ice rattled against his teeth as he remembered the scene in his bedroom. What had his mother wanted to tell him? He jerked his head up and his mouth fell open as he stared over the crowd of diners. Had she been about to explain the truth about his father?

At the next table, a little kid was throwing a tantrum. "I wanna hot dog!" the kid yelled. "Don't like chicken! I wanna go home!" He flung out an arm, knocking over a carton of milk. Neil watched the milk spread across the tabletop and flow down into a stroller beside the mother's chair.

He turned his eyes away and slumped in his seat. His mom hadn't been about to tell him any such thing. She probably just wanted to explain how to hang a picture properly. She had looked pretty stunned though, he thought, as she sat there on the bed. Maybe the painting had upset her for some reason, but he couldn't imagine why.

"Lemme go!" The kid was being was hauled off, his fat little legs flailing under his dad's arm. The woman hunched over the crying baby, trying to mop up the spilled milk with a handful of brown paper napkins. Neil shoved his plate away. Even a super-annoying kid like that had a father who was willing to put up with him. He put his head in his hands and closed his eyes, trying to think of somewhere to go.

He opened his eyes a few minutes later and looked around sleepily, then something made him sit upright. Was that Courtenay coming through the street door into the food court? It sure looked like her coat, and her pale face and dark hair. He stood up to get a better look. It was definitely her, he could see now. She looked just as fed up as he felt, walking slowly past the tables, head down. He waved his whole arm to get her attention.

The kid, back again and clutching a squeezy ketchup bottle, stared at him, his mucky mouth hanging open. He was pretty amazed himself. He, Neil MacLeod, standing up in a public place and waving madly to attract the attention of a cool girl! As she walked on, he went even further and yelled across the tables, "Hey, Courtenay!"

She stopped and looked around, confused, until she recognized him. Eyebrows up, she grinned and made her way to his table. Keeping her coat well clear of the kid, she flopped down opposite him.

"Hey!" she said. "How's it going, Neil?"

"Good." His voice came out in a squawk.

"What are you doing here?"

He shrugged. "Dunno. Nothing I guess."

"Same as me, then." She smiled. "Hey, I was just talking to your grandmother this afternoon, believe it or not."

He liked her voice. It was clear and soft, not like that scratchy voice a lot of girls had, like it was being dragged from the back of a very sore throat.

"How come you were talking to my grandmother?" he asked.

"I went to tell her I was running away, because, like I told you, she's kind of a friend of mine. Anyway, she persuaded me not to go right away. She said I should try to talk to my mom and dad first. So I went back home and made a yummy spaghetti sauce for supper with stuff from the fridge. You know, a real family meal. Then my mom texted me she was going out with"— she rolled her eyes—"'the girls,' and she might stay over at her friend's house since it was Friday night." She shrugged. "My dad was going to be out too, so I came here, looking for someone to hang out with."

Neil leaned back, squinting at Courtenay over his Coke with what he hoped was a worldly look. "Will I do?"

"I guess." The silver bead on her lip flashed as she gave him a crooked little closed-mouth smile.

They sat across the table, grinning at each other. Her eyebrows were thin, lively arcs and her mouth, with its upturned corners, made her look like she often said funny things. She had a small gap between her very white front teeth. He glanced again at the silver stud on her lower lip. She must have easygoing parents, he thought.

"Tell you what," she said. "Why don't you come home with me, and we can have an all-you-can-eat spaghetti supper?" She pushed his plastic plate away with a chipped purple fingernail. "It'll be better than this junk, that's for sure."

"Sounds great," said Neil, trying not to show his relief. At least now he had someplace to go.

chapter 5

NEIL TWIRLED THE LAST DELICIOUS forkful of spaghetti onto his spoon and crammed it into his mouth.

"So, you don't know anything at all about your father?" Courtenay asked.

"Nothing," he said. "I've asked a million times, but she won't tell me anything."

Courtenay stood to collect their bowls. "But you must know something. Like, what's his name, for a start?"

"All I know is that his name is Adam, and that he vanished before I was born."

"But if he deserted you and your mother like that, why would you want to find him?"

He picked up the salad bowl. "I need to know who he is, or was. I just feel sort of incomplete, not even knowing that."

"But you must know *something*, Neil. Like, what did he do?" She walked into the kitchen, and Neil followed her.

"Oh, he was an artist like my mom," he said. "I know that much."

"So, you're right," she said, stacking dishes in the sink. "You don't know much at all."

"Yes, and it's really freaking me out. There's only me and my mom in my whole family, apart from this grandmother I've just met. But there is one thing," he said, lifting a finger at her to wait. He retrieved the shopping bag from the dining room. "At least now I've got this." He pulled out the painting. "Ta-da!"

Courtenay's eyebrows shot up and then lowered in a frown as she peered at the painting. "But isn't that the picture from next door?" She looked up. "How come you've got it?"

"Margaret gave it to me. It's by my father."

"What? Your father painted this?" She looked from him to the painting and back. "That's awesome, Neil."

"What do you think of it?" He fixed her with his eyes. "Just out of curiosity, how does it make you feel?"

She cocked her head to one side and squinted at it. "I never really looked at it before," she said. "It was sort of in the dark there and, you know, out of the way, but it kind of scares me now that I can really see it. It makes me feel like something's trapped in there and fighting to get out. That sort of torn-looking red bit there in the middle especially."

"I know," he said, happy that she saw it too. "That's what I think too. It's like it's shouting at me and wants something from me."

"Put it back in the bag, Neil, please. It's creeping me out." She grabbed the bag and held it open so he could shove the painting back inside, then propped it against the couch on the other side of the dining room.

"Before we have dessert," she said, "I want to tell you something your grandma told me after school today."

He watched her take two steaming domes out of the microwave, turn them out into bowls and then spoon the hot, runny syrup over them. "What did she tell you?"

"She said that her son disappeared at pretty much the same time her husband took off."

"Her *what*? Her son disappeared? But that would mean my mom has a brother," Neil said, trying to figure it out in his head. "So on top of having a father that disappeared, a grandfather that took off, and a brand-new grandmother, now I have a disappearing uncle too? I don't believe this. Can you believe it?"

"I believe she has a son, Neil, and that she somehow lost him, and that she wishes they'd been able to talk about the problem, whatever it was. She still misses them both a lot, I think. She tries to hide it, but she's a very sad and lonely lady."

"I think you're right about that," Neil said as they sat back down at the table. "She showed me a photo of her husband, Ken, and I figured she was still upset about him taking off. She told me I looked a bit like him, but I couldn't see that from the photos. She didn't show me pics of any son, though. I wonder why not. Is he dead, do you think?"

"I don't think so, but it's definitely weird." She plopped a scoop of ice cream onto his dessert.

"Maybe she just wanted you to focus on your grandfather. Like, you know, one new relative at a time sort of thing."

"I guess so. You're probably right."

The dessert was incredible: hot, fluffy, cakey stuff soaked in syrup. He'd never tasted anything like it.

"So what about your mom?" asked Courtenay. "Won't she be worrying about you?" She waved her spoon in the air and laughed. "Mine's not going to be bothering herself about me tonight, that's for sure."

Neil thought about how his mom had always watched over him. She always waited for him to come home, and worried over every little scrape and sniffle. Lately she'd been driving him crazy with all her questions and worrying. He remembered how pale she'd turned when he yelled at her in his bedroom.

"She'll be worrying for sure," he said.

Courtenay looked at him in surprise. "Doesn't that bother you?"

He shrugged. "She doesn't seem to care how worried *I* am. So why should I care about her?" He took another mouthful as a phone started ringing in the distance.

"That's Margaret's phone next door," Courtenay said. "You can hear everything through these walls." She turned back to her pudding.

A comfortable silence followed, broken only by the clacking of spoons, until the ringing started up again. Courtenay looked at Neil, her eyes wide. "I'll bet that's your mom phoning Margaret, looking for you," she said. "Now Margaret will be worried sick too." She jabbed her spoon towards him. "You really should call her, Neil. Tell her you're okay, and not to worry. Tell her you'll be home when you feel like it."

He turned his phone back on and found four text messages, all from his mom.

Call me and I'll come and get you wherever you are

Come home Neil and I'll tell you everything right away I promise

Neil I'm so sorry. Please PLEASE call me!

The last one was longer.

I don't know what to do Neil, but I'll drive around until I find you. I'll stay out all night if I have to.

"She's worried all right." He held out the phone for Courtenay to read, and was surprised to see her face crumple and turn pink as she took in the messages.

She raised tear-filled eyes to his. "Do you have any clue how lucky you are to be cared about like this? Nobody has ever felt like that about me. And if they did, they sure don't anymore." She sniffed. "Somebody must have once, though, I guess, or I wouldn't know what I was missing, would I?" She blew her nose on her napkin. "Come on, Neil. Call your mom and put her out of her misery. Go on, call her!"

He sighed, then poked at his cellphone and listened. "She's not answering."

"Well, leave a message!"

"I'm fine," he texted, his fingers clumsy on the keyboard. "*Sorry.*"

As Neil scraped up the last of the syrup, his cellphone rang.

"Hello?" he asked. He expected to hear his mother's angry voice, but to his surprise, it was Margaret.

"Oh, Neil!" Her voice sounded old and shaky. "I'm so happy you answered! Where are you?"

"I'm just next door with Courtenay, actually. Why? What's up?"

"Oh, thank God! Come quickly. The police are waiting to take us to the hospital."

"The hospital?" he asked, an uneasy feeling creeping up on him.

"There's been an accident," said Margaret. "It's your mother."

chapter 6

THE WAITING ROOM IN THE INTENSIVE
care unit was weirdly peaceful. In fact, it
felt a bit like being in church. Neil had imagined a scene of bloodstained chaos: gurneys
hurtling past, pushed by sprinting orderlies;
doctors and nurses giving quick treatment to
mangled bodies; doors swinging open to show
surgeons standing at the ready. But here, apart
from the murmur of the overhead TV, everything was silent.

He poked his head into the hallway. The floor was a shining stretch of beige tiles. Posters on the mauve and pale-green walls showed confident-looking nurses and doctors smiling down at equally happy patients. *We're here for you*, the posters declared in English and French.

Feeling cold and sick to his stomach, he clasped his trembling hands together.

Constable Gauvreau, who had driven them to the hospital, came stomping back into the waiting room. His large dark form and loud voice were shocking in the still, pale room. He handed Neil a Styrofoam cup. "Hot chocolate," he said. "I've got a boy about your age and he can't get enough of the stuff."

Neil clutched the hot drink gratefully. "Thanks," he said. He looked up into the officer's kind, broad face and, to his embarrassment, realized that his eyes were filling with tears.

"Hey there, don't be upset," said Constable Gauvreau. He sat down next to Neil and clapped a firm hand on his shoulder. "The staff here are terrific. Your mom's in good hands."

Neil squinted up at the cop, wondering if he was just saying that to make him feel better. The warm smile he received reassured him a little bit.

"Thanks" he said again, unable to come up with anything else.

The constable stood and had a quick, quiet conversation with Neil's grandmother. Then, with a final tip of his hat, he left. The sound of his steady footsteps receded down the hallway.

Neil's grandmother gave him a tight smile and looked away. He slumped in his chair. This accident was all his fault. He'd deliberately turned off his cellphone so his mom couldn't call him, which was why she'd gone rushing around looking for him. Her text messages showed how frantic she'd been. What if she was seriously hurt? What if...? There were pins and needles in his stomach and a pain in his chest. He swallowed and looked again at his grandmother, but her eyes were closed.

With a squeak of rubber on vinyl, a pretty, dark-haired nurse hovered in the doorway. "Good news!" she said, smiling at them. "Ms. MacLeod's condition has stabilized. We'll be able to tell you more soon. I'm Julie, by the way. I'll be looking after Ms. MacLeod." She smiled again before hurrying off down the hall.

"Oh, thank God!" said Margaret. She leaned her head back and looked up at the ceiling, her thin lips moving slightly. Was she praying?

Neil studied her pale, lined face. Could she have been thinking his mom might actually die? She couldn't die. She was all he had. And she loved him. And he loved her. His chin started wobbling.

Margaret opened her eyes and smiled at him. "This really is good news, Neil," she said. "It sounds as if your mom's going to pull through."

He sat up. "What do you mean? Were you afraid she wouldn't?"

She looked away at his question and pursed her lips. "Yes, I was," she said after a pause. "She was seriously injured. One has to be prepared."

"Didn't I have to be prepared? She is my mother after all," he said. "Shouldn't *I* have been told how serious it was?"

"I don't think so, Neil. Not until we knew what we were talking about. There was no need to frighten you unnecessarily."

Louder squeaks could be heard coming down the hallway before a short, square woman with hair like grated carrots and sharp green eyes marched in, a clipboard in her hands.

"I take it you are, er"—with raised eyebrows and her mouth pulled down, she checked her notes—"Ms. MacLeod's mother and son?"

His grandmother nodded stiffly.

"I'm Sister Vincent." She glanced at her watch. "Now, here's the situation." Her eyes went back to the clipboard. "The patient has sustained a head injury, and is still unconscious. The MRI shows a small fracture of the skull but no displacement."

Neil gulped. Wasn't a fractured skull pretty serious?

"There is some swelling of the brain," the Sister continued, "but it seems to be levelling off and hopefully will go down." She tucked the clipboard under her arm and straightened her white coat, then turned to walk down the hall. "You may see the patient for five minutes, *if* there is no disturbance."

Why was she being so stern? Neil wondered. It wasn't as if his mother had done this to herself, or on purpose.

Over her shoulder, she added, "Now, if you'll follow me." They trailed obediently after her down the hall.

Three patients lay in separate areas of the room on complicated metal beds, each with a bank of machinery at its head. On Neil's right an old man lay as if dead, his purple mouth hanging open in a putty-coloured face. Beyond him, a white mound gurgled and groaned. In the third bed, a thin form lay straight and still, almost flat, under the sheets, its profile sharp and yellowish below the bandages. Could that seriously be his mother?

Machines clicked and buzzed as Neil and his grandmother approached the bed. A thin tube ran down to the forearm from a clear plastic bag dangling above. Neil turned his eyes from another bag, half-filled with yellow liquid, hanging below the bed, to stare at the bruised, closed eyes, so naked-looking without makeup; and at the head, bandaged in a sort of turban that hid all signs of hair. Another bandage crossed the nose and cheekbones. The thin lips were pale. It could have been anybody. In fact, looking at the dead-pale mouth, he thought for a moment that this wasn't his mother after all—she always wore dark red lipstick—but his grandmother seemed sure.

Taking one of Neil's mom's hands in hers, Margaret motioned to him to go around the bed to take the other.

"Mom's here," she said softly, leaning over. "And Neil. We're right beside you, Sasha. You're going to be fine."

Margaret glanced across the bed, waiting

for him to say something. Neil stared down at the alien shape of his mother, felt her cold, unmoving hand in his, but couldn't think of what to say.

Finally, he leaned forward and stared down at her. "I'm sorry," he said. "I'm really sorry, Mom."

***

The next morning, while his grandmother sat patiently waiting for the specialist to come and give the latest report on his mother's condition, Neil explored the halls of the ICU.

He walked past a row of steel-mesh trolleys lining the wall, some holding clean, neatly folded bedding wrapped in clear blue plastic; others loaded with transparent yellow bags of dirty linen. He went by recycling bins, washrooms, and a recessed fire extinguisher, until he was faced by a steel door marked *Restricted Access, Authorized Personnel Only*.

He took the elevator down to the ground floor and wandered along until he came across the hospital gift shop. He looked around, hoping to find something to give his mom when she woke up. He breathed in the scented air. Everything in here seemed aimed at women, he thought. Didn't men get sick?

He surveyed the shelves of toiletries and the sappy cards and *Get Well Soon* balloons, and gawked at the price of the refrigerated flower arrangements. He skimmed over the titles in a rack of magazines, but saw nothing that would interest her. Another rack of schmaltzy-looking paperbacks looked just as unsuitable.

He picked up a Perkins-type kitten from amongst the stuffed animals, then put it back and turned to study a shelf of candles shaped like praying hands. On the shelf above, smiling china angels held out their palms in blessing over miniature curling stones bearing messages like, *All Things are Possible with God* and *Prayer is the Answer*. He moved on to read the framed *Serenity Prayer* which looked good to him, although he wasn't quite sure his mom would appreciate it.

He knew she wouldn't like the scarves either, or the jewelry, even if he could afford them. Nothing in here would suit her.

Across the hall, he saw a little coffee shop where worried-looking people sat at small tables, clutching mugs or easing plastic film off their muffins. *Try Our New Green Apple Smoothie!* said a big notice standing on the floor by the entrance. It was tempting, but he remembered his mom and left the cafeteria to follow the red line on the floor and the lists and arrows on the walls back to the ICU.

His grandmother was not in the waiting room. Had something happened? There was no one around, and Neil suddenly felt frightened. He set off quickly for his mom's room. At the door he slowed down, worried at what he might find. He took a deep breath and then stepped into the room.

"Hello, sweetie!" His mom, just barely lifting her head, put out her hand to him and smiled. She looked very strange without her makeup and long hair, but her eyes had the same loving look.

He bent forward to kiss her pale, unscented cheek, a lump in his throat. "I was so scared, Mom!" he said. "I feel so bad about causing your accident!"

"Shush now," she said, with a weak smile. "I caused it myself with my stupid panicking." Her eyelids drooped and fluttered.

"That's enough now," the ginger-headed Sister said, ushering him out. "Time to go."

chapter 7

"WE CAN ALWAYS GO BACK TO THE townhouse to get anything you want while you stay with me," Neil's grandmother said, squinting through the clunking wipers of her old Honda as they drove back to her house. "I don't think it will be too long until your mom's well enough to leave the hospital."

He thought how weak and alien his mother had looked that afternoon. Without her makeup on and with her hair shaved off, she was hard to recognize. Remembering the photograph, he turned to his grandmother and opened his mouth to ask if his mom had ever had a brother, but shut it, seeing the tired look on her face as she stared at the road ahead.

After dinner they stood in the little spare bedroom looking at the painting; Neil had fetched it from Courtenay's and propped it up on the chest of drawers.

"So, it's come back home," he said to Margaret. He saw how it seemed to take over this little room, the way it had dominated his bedroom in the new house. "Why was it in your house, anyway?" he asked.

She looked away. "Your mother gave it to me."

That made sense. His mom never liked to even think about his father, let alone talk about him, so she certainly wouldn't have wanted such a reminder in her own house. But when could she have given it to Margaret? And why would his grandmother have wanted it? Wouldn't she have been mad at her daughter's husband for disappearing like that, abandoning his wife and unborn baby? He shrugged, feeling very tired. Whatever the story, the painting was staying with him.

Courtenay came to Margaret's door after school the next day. She fumbled around in her backpack as she came in and then handed Neil a dark blue, hardback book. "Here, give this back to your grandma, would you? She lent it to me."

The book, *Great Expectations* by Charles Dickens, looked awfully long. He flipped through the pages. It even smelled old, but he saw it had lots of interesting black and white illustrations.

"Is it good?" he asked.

"It's amazing! You should try it." She hesitated. "If you like reading, that is."

"It's what I do, mostly, other than the art stuff."

She narrowed her eyes at him. "What have you read?"

"Well, I just finished *A Wrinkle in Time*. And I've read the *Narnia* books, and all the *Harry Potter* books, of course, and some Isaac Asimov, and *The Golden Compass* and the rest of that series, and—"

"Okay, okay! I'm convinced," she said, grinning. "If you can read those, you can manage this one. Honestly, once I started it, I couldn't put it down." She took off her coat. "How's your mom?"

"She's getting better, but she's been having bad headaches, so they're keeping her in for observation a couple of days longer."

"That's too bad about the headaches, but it's good she's getting better. And how about you? Are you okay?"

"I guess, but I'm worried about my mom, and I'm feeling kind of mixed up these days," he said. Courtenay frowned sympathetically.

In the kitchen, he held out the big round tin full of homemade peanut-butter cookies Margaret had left out for him.

"The thing is," he said, selecting a cookie, "it's not knowing who my father is that makes me feel like a total nobody. If I don't know who *he* is, I don't know who *I* am. I'm like a tree with only one branch. Do you see what I mean?"

She gave him a sideways look. "Actually, I don't see what you mean, Neil. What about your mom? If you're a branch, then she's the trunk of your tree. How can that be nothing?"

"Oh, you know," he said, "Neil, *nil*, *null and void*. Even my name means *nothing*."

She rolled her eyes. "Gimme a break. Neil's an okay name, isn't it? It's good. It's, like, strong and straightforward. What's wrong with that?"

She pulled out her phone. After a quick search she held it out to him. "See, you're talking total crap. Neil's an old Irish name, and it means *champion*. That's like the opposite of nothing."

Neil opened his mouth but closed it again. She was kind of hard to argue with.

"Anyway," she went on, "why does it matter what your name was supposed to mean, like, a thousand years ago? You can't seriously believe it has any effect on your personality or on your fate?"

"Guess not," he said with a shrug.

While Courtenay went back to fiddling on her phone, Neil picked up the book and examined the first illustration: a boy in the clutches of a terrifying man, next to an old tombstone. This he had to read.

She held her phone out. "Look. Mine means *court attendant*, or *brave*." She laughed. "I think I'll settle for brave. Court attendant would probably mean something like 'gofer' in a law office today."

She drained her glass of milk, wiping off the white moustache with the back of her hand. "Margaret's so nice to leave homemade cookies like this. You're so lucky to have her for your grandma."

"Do you have a grandmother?" he asked. She seemed kind of lonely, he thought. It sounded like her parents were out an awful lot.

"My mom's mom is dead, and my dad's mom lives in Florida with her new boyfriend. She doesn't want to see us anymore, not since my mom got drunk and was rude about them living in a trailer."

"Your mom gets drunk?" He could hardly imagine such a thing. Moms were supposed to stay home when they weren't working, and look after everything.

"Whatever." She checked the weight of the carton before pouring herself another couple of inches of milk. "She has bad nerves and says it helps her relax." She shrugged. "At least she's better than my dad."

"What do you mean?" He was even more shocked. "Is he...?"

"Nah, he's all right. It's just he has stupid friends. They both do, if you ask me."

"Do your parents, like, fight and stuff?"

"Well, not in public. They've both got good jobs, well my mom does anyway, and they go to work every day, so I guess in the evenings and on weekends they feel like having a good time."

"But do they ever, you know," he didn't know how to put this, "hurt you?"

"Oh no. They mostly ignore me. And I ignore them. I can't wait to grow up and live on my own."

To change the subject, he picked up *Great Expectations*. "What's this about anyway?"

"Oh, it's about a boy who gets everything dead wrong and learns the hard way which end is up."

"What's happening in this picture?" He showed her the illustration.

"Why don't you read it to find out?" she said, smirking. Then her face got serious. "But seriously, what's all that about a 'nothing' background, Neil? I mean, lots of kids don't know who their father is, or if they do, they might seriously prefer not to. See, I think we just are who we are. That's all there is to it. You're just you, and you're okay. You're smart, and," she shrugged and pulled her crooked little grin, "not bad-looking. And I can see from the cover of your notebook over there that you can draw awesome horses!"

Neil felt himself go red. He thought of himself as a nerd, and maybe a bit of a loner. But Courtenay thought he was "smart and not bad-looking." He stood up straighter.

"You don't have to be like your father or your mother at all," she went on. "Or you can just choose to take the best bits. Like, you're good at art for instance. You got that from your parents." She took another cookie.

He thought about it. "What are the best bits for you then?" he asked.

She swallowed. "Hah! That's a tough one!" She took another bite. "Best bits? Well, I guess my dad can be pretty funny, and my mom is real smart."

"Well you're funny and smart," he said, "and at least you have the two of them. Not like me."

She brushed a few crumbs off her coat. "I tell you what, Neil," she said, looking up, "personally, I don't think you're missing much, but since you want to find your dad so bad, you'd better just get on with it. Make like a detective and do what you can to find stuff out for yourself." She grabbed her backpack, and before she left turned back to say, "Give me a shout if you want any help."

chapter 8

WHEN NEIL GOT HOME FROM SCHOOL the next day, he found a note on the kitchen table from Margaret: *Gone to see Sasha and do some shopping. Back around 6:30*. He looked at his watch. It was nearly 4:00. He had the house to himself for over two hours. Plenty of time to do some detective work. Maybe Courtenay could come over and help him look for evidence. He got out his cellphone and texted her. She answered immediately: she'd be right over.

While he waited for her, he looked through Margaret's desk and cabinet for documents or photographs but found nothing useful. Through the window, he saw Courtenay turn onto the garden path.

"We're going to look for pictures," he told her as she took off her coat. "I've already done the downstairs."

"Cool!" she said. "Let's go."

Neil felt kind of guilty about trespassing as they went upstairs to Margaret's bedroom, but it was the only way to find any clues. Careful not to disturb anything, they searched her closet and looked under her bed, and then checked out her chest of drawers. There, finally, under some sweaters in the bottom drawer, they found a photo album.

They sat at the dinner table, the album spread before them, and flipped through several pages of old photos until they came to some of a girl with dark hair waving back from a point on her forehead who they agreed had to be Margaret.

Several pages later, the photo of Ken with the horse appeared. "That's my grandfather, Ken," Neil told Courtenay, who studied it with interest. "And that's his horse, Dude. I wonder why Ken went off like that," he said. "And why my mom's never even mentioned him."

"Sure is strange." Courtenay turned the page. "Hey, look at this!"

They saw a whole bunch of photos of what had to be his mom as a baby, mostly with Margaret and Ken, all three looking totally happy. On the next page was a studio portrait of baby Sasha, at about one year old.

"Aw, she's so cute!" Courtenay said.

He examined the photo carefully. She was certainly cute enough, sitting up all big eyes and dark curls, wearing stripy overalls and holding a teddy bear. As they turned the pages, they saw that the curls were gone, and she was a crop-haired toddler in dungarees, then a leggy little kid in shorts and T-shirts. And then, it seemed, there were no more photos of Sasha. Frowning, they turned the pages, peering closely at the pictures.

"Who is this other kid, anyway?" Courtenay said.

"Not my mom, anyway," Neil said, looking at the bullet-headed, knobbly-kneed, sulky-looking kid, "since it's obviously a boy." He looked up at Courtenay. "Hey! This has gotta be my missing uncle."

"Right! Of course." said Courtenay.

"He's definitely one of the family," Neil said. "He's got the widow's peak for one thing, and the tall skinny build, like my mom and Margaret."

They turned several more pages, seeing many more photos of that boy alone or with his parents, but none of Sasha.

"What do you think's going on here?" Neil said. "Where's my mom in all this?"

"Beats me," Courtenay said. "So weird."

Neil narrowed his eyes at a shot of the boy, now a teenager in a high school graduation gown and flat hat, scowling between a proud-looking Margaret and the ever-smiling Ken. "If this guy is my mom's brother, I wonder why he always looks so down," he said.

A couple of pages later, they found a university graduation portrait of the same guy; his long hair made the likeness to his mom even more striking.

"Maybe he and my mom were twins," Neil said. "They look almost exactly alike."

"Totally," she agreed.

He looked at her, surprised. "You've met my mom?"

"Yeah," she said, reaching past him to turn the page. "Here at Margaret's. A couple of times. She's really nice."

Neil shifted uncomfortably at the mention of his grandmother. "Margaret might be home from the hospital soon," he said. "I really don't want her to know I was going through her stuff."

Courtenay ignored him. She was staring intently at the university graduation photo of the secret uncle.

"This is kind of freaking me out, Neil," she said. "This guy could, like, totally *be* your mom."

He saw her wide-open blue eyes with their thick black lashes, and her half-open pink mouth with the shiny silver ball on the lower lip. Then he looked again at the brooding, handsome face in the photo.

"You've got to go," he said suddenly, slamming the album shut. "Now! Before Margaret gets back. Hurry up. She'll be here any minute."

"Wait a minute—you said she wouldn't be home until 6:30."

"Go on," he said, pointing at the door. "Grab your stuff and get out of here!"

Courtenay stared at him with a mix of anger and confusion. Then she turned and grabbed her coat and backpack and went out, slamming the door.

He didn't know why he'd been so rude to her. Margaret wouldn't really be back for a while. He'd just suddenly known that he had to be alone with this. Something was seriously wrong here, and he had to figure it out by himself. He had a scared, trembly feeling, and his mind was whirling: Sasha, uncle, brother, twin, secret.... That was it. There was a secret here, and he had to figure it out. But why was he so scared?

He did some deep breathing, the way his mom had shown him, trying to think about his breath and nothing else.

When he could think more clearly, he blew his nose and shook back his hair and opened the album again. There was still a chance that some picture he hadn't seen yet would make sense of it all. With trembling fingers, he flipped back to the last photo they'd seen, the guy's graduation picture, and then turned the page.

A black and white studio portrait of two people lay in front of him: the mystery man and a girl, their heads together, smiling up at him. Underneath was written, *Adam and Jessica*.

But that was his father's name: *Adam*! Neil looked again at the date: two years before he was born. What could this possibly mean? As he struggled with these questions, his eyes turned to the girl's face and opened wide.

All thoughts of his father fell away as he stared. Knees shaking, he reached for a chair. The girl was new to him, and yet she was startlingly, shockingly familiar.

He knew that face. He knew those eyes were a light, bright blue. He knew how that fair, curly hair would feel in his fingers, softly crunchy and springy. He knew how soft those lips were, and what it was like to be held, warm and safe, in those arms. He thought he could smell a flowery scent, and he knew that just under her blouse, in the hollow above her collarbone, was a small, brown mole.

When he could breathe properly again, and the dizzy feeling went off, he looked once more at her picture and then up at the shadowy ceiling. Something in him, he realized, a long-buried part, had known this truth all along. No wonder he was overwhelmed sometimes by a sadness he couldn't explain. As he looked at the soft, delicate face of his birth mother, tears welled up and ran down his cheeks.

The startling swish of a passing car reminded Neil that Margaret would be back before long. He stared again at the photo of the girl. Since she was definitely his mother, then that guy, Adam, was probably his father. So who was Sasha? His aunt? He just couldn't understand it. None of it made sense.

He turned back to the picture of the man and saw again the uncanny resemblance to Sasha. He made himself sit still and concentrate. How likely was it that his mother had an identical twin brother that she had somehow forgotten to mention? Why were there no pictures of her in the album?

His mouth was dry, and his heart was beating so loudly he could hear it. He studied the man's features again, and this time he saw his mother in every detail: in the dark, downward-sloping eyes, in the wide mouth, strong nose and chin, and in the thick wavy hair springing from the so-familiar point in the forehead, even in the challenging expression.

He closed his eyes, his head and heart pounding and a sick feeling in his stomach.

Adam was Sasha, and Sasha was Adam—or at least, she had been at one time.

So, here was the truth. The mystery was solved. Sasha was not his mother, Jessica was. And there was no father to find. No father at all, not anymore.

What did this make him? he wondered, an orphan? No, not even that. Was there even a word for what he was? No wonder he felt like a nobody.

A huge anger rose in him. He grabbed the big black kitchen scissors. Holding his breath and trying to steady his hands, he cut out the picture of Jessica. Then, picking up Adam's picture with the tips of his fingers, he slowly tore it in half; then, working faster and faster, he ripped it into smaller and smaller pieces. He threw the fragments into the garbage. Using the potato masher, he rammed them into the mess of leftover porridge, lasagna, and oily salad scraps.

He folded Jessica's picture and slipped it into the back pocket of his jeans. Then he flipped back to the beginning of the album and pulled out and cut up every single photo of the boy. He slammed the book shut, ran upstairs to his bedroom, and flung the painting down onto the bed.

"I *hate* you! I *hate* you! I *hate* you!" He raised the pointed scissors over the painting's blood-red heart. He lifted his hand even higher, but stopped with a dry sob. Lowering his arm, he dropped the weapon with a clatter and swept the painting onto the floor.

He had to get out of there. Disappear completely. The picture of Ken and the horse flashed into his mind and he made his decision.

He looked at his watch. Margaret would be back any minute. He stuffed his backpack with clothes and then checked his money. There was barely enough for a meal. In the entryway, he found his mother's purse, which Margaret had taken home from the hospital. He pulled out all the cash from her wallet, along with her credit card. He knew her pin number off by heart: a combination of his birth year and hers.

As the beams from Margaret's car lit the mountain ash tree in the back parking lot, he grabbed his backpack and rain slicker, struggled into his boots, and ran out into the street, leaving the front door open behind him.

chapter 9

*A*FTER A LONG, COLD WALK, NEIL arrived at the bus station. He looked around, not sure where to go or what to do next. It was seven-thirty and dark. He saw a bus roll into the lot, while people waited in line at a door for another bus idling outside.

He spotted the words *Customer Service Office*, and made for the window beneath.

"Can you tell me how to get to Saint John, New Brunswick?" he asked the blond girl at the counter.

"Wow! That's quite a trek you're looking at there, handsome!" she said. She typed something into her keyboard. "It'll take you at least twenty-two hours by bus, with four changes: at Montreal, Quebec City, Edmundston, and Woodstock." She gave him a sharp look. "Do your parents know you're doing this?"

"Yes, of course. I'm going to visit my grand-father. He's expecting me."

"I see." She glanced at her computer screen while making some notes. "That bus waiting over there will be boarding for Montreal in a few min-utes," she said.

"I'll take it," he said quickly. "Thanks."

At the ATM he guiltily used his mother's credit card to take out the huge sum of three hun-dred dollars. He bought his ticket and joined the lineup for the Montreal bus.

By the time he got on, all the seats were taken except for one, next to an old woman.

"Going to Montreal?" the woman asked as he sat down.

"Uh huh," he said, not wanting to give away any secrets.

She nodded and went back to her Sudoku.

As Neil looked around, he saw that nearly everyone was on their phones, although a few were reading. He realized that in his rush, he had left *Great Expectations* behind, and his phone was nearly dead. Luckily he had his sketch pad and pencil set, but that was no good on a moving bus. Suddenly feeling very tired, Neil closed his eyes and tried to make his mind blank. He felt the vibration and jolt as the bus moved out onto the road, and before long they were rolling along the highway, leaving Ottawa behind.

***

The next thing Neil knew, the bus had arrived at the Montreal station.

The old woman waved goodbye as she and the other passengers left. Feeling very lonely, he waved back.

The quiet, almost empty station where he would spend the next few hours smelled of gas and oil and stale food. At the miraculously still-open Subway, he bought a pepperoni sub, a bag of salt and vinegar chips, and a bottle of 7Up. He wolfed down the lot and looked at his watch. All of ten minutes had passed.

Here was a chance, though, to do some draw-ing. He got his supplies out and began making sketches of the few people still around. First, he tried drawing a baby, fast asleep in its stroller, but its blobby face was impossible to capture. He did better on a sketch of a stout old woman, nodding sleepily and ringed by bulging bags that echoed her shape. He finally focused on a slim, dark-eyed girl in a hijab, lost in thought. He got so caught up in showing the flow of her clothes and the shadows of her face that the next thing he knew, it was time to get on the Quebec City bus.

As soon as the bus got onto the highway, Neil took the photo from his jeans pocket. This was his real mother, he thought: Jessica, gentle and sweet and pretty, not Sasha. He drank in the curve of Jessica's cheek, the soft shine of her eyes, the way her blond curls shone in the light, his mind coming up with a few uncertain memories: fine, soft, sky-blue material with small raised white dots; that flowery scent; a high sweet voice singing a song with the word "sleep" in it; a man's voice shouting; the sound of crying; a dark, narrow staircase.

Aware that the guy next to him was looking at him nervously, Neil turned his face to the window to conceal his tears. His breath came in little gasps and his shoulders shook as his reflection stared back, hollow-eyed, from the dark glass.

Once he got a grip on himself, he blew his nose and sat up straight. The first thing he'd do after he reached his grandfather, he decided, would be to look for Jessica. Maybe he could get some clue from Ken about where to start looking. Then he would make a plan.

He wondered what had happened to Jessica. Had that Sasha/Adam person, who Jessica probably thought was going to marry her, totally abandoned her and the unborn baby that was going to be him? Had she/he lied to Jessica, too? How was he supposed to think of his mom now? As his lying mother? Or as his lying father?

He couldn't get his head around it. He decided to block his so-called mother from his mind, refuse to think about her. If he ever did think of her, it would be as *Sasha*, not *Mom*. Never again Mom. He would just forget all about her and join the rest of the disappearing men in his family. He would be the disappearing boy, and start a whole new life, like Ken had.

***

Some time later, Neil was awakened from a fitful nap. The blond, muscular-looking guy next to him put down his textbook and held out a zip-lock bag.

"Hey man, want a brownie? My girlfriend's a great cook."

"Hey, thanks a lot." Neil helped himself to a large fresh square. It tasted almost as good as his...Sasha's.

Even though he'd made up his mind to forget her, images of Sasha kept forcing their way into Neil's head: how she'd looked getting into the car that last morning, wearing her royal-blue slicker and waving goodbye, all excited about her new job at the hospital; how she'd appeared later, sitting on his bed, staring white-faced at the painting; and how helpless, even lifeless, she'd seemed, lying in the hospital.

He shook his head and took another bite of his brownie. "This is great, "he said. "Thanks."

"No problem." The guy grinned. "Happy to share. Have another." He held out the bag. "You going far?"

"I'm going to visit my grandfather," Neil said, eagerly helping himself. "He has a stable near Saint John."

"Wow! Long trip, eh? I'm getting off at Quebec City myself. Can you ride a horse?"

"No, but he's going to teach me."

"Cool! How long are you going for?"

He should never have gotten into this. "I don't know," he said. "Depends how things work out."

The guy nodded, then opened his book. "Gotta study," he said. "Big test next week."

Fortified by the brownies and the company, Neil watched the fields and woods fly by and imagined himself riding a fine horse like the one in the photo.

At the Quebec station, he had just enough time to buy a comic and a Coke before boarding the bus to Edmundston.

Judging by the times on the ticket, he was in for another long haul. He was already sick to death of travelling. He wished he had something to do or to read, and once again regretted leaving Margaret's book behind.

He'd never see Margaret again either, he thought sadly as the bus took him further east. But he'd have a grandfather, and a fun one at that. They'd have a love of horses in common, and he knew that his grandfather would be happy to teach him to ride.

He looked out the window. Lots of nothing. No snow-capped mountains, no glittering sea, just endless fields and hills and woods, becoming more visible in the dawning light.

"Mind if I sit here?" A girl, probably about seventeen, plonked herself down on the empty seat beside him. She hadn't given him much choice, but she was pretty, with long shiny brown hair and big, blue-gray eyes.

"Fine by me," he said.

"There's a guy back there who keeps hitting on me," she whispered, "I can't get him to leave me alone. I told him you're my brother. Okay?"

He nodded. "Sure." He half stood and turned to look to the back of the half-empty bus. "Where's he sitting?"

She pulled him down. "Don't look! I said you were my big brother just to scare him off. You look pretty tall from the back."

"Okay, but if I'm supposed to be your brother, why weren't you already sitting with me?"

"We didn't get into that, but we can make it up if you like." She smiled and narrowed her eyes at him. "Why do you think?"

He sat back and closed his eyes, considering. "Hmm. I think you wanted to sit next to the handsome dude back there in the black leather jacket," he said, "and told your brother to get lost."

She laughed. "Aren't you cheeky! What's your name? I'm Maddie."

"I'm Neil." He looked sideways at her. "Where are we now?"

"Edmundston's the next stop. That's where I live. You?"

"I'm going on to Saint John." He frowned. Where's the dude getting off, do you know?"

"He said Edmundston."

"Is someone meeting you there?" he asked.

"Yes. My actual big brother is supposed to meet me there. I hope he's not late." She shivered. "To be honest, that guy scares me."

"Don't worry, Maddie," he said, feeling very big and strong. "I'll hang around the station with you if you like. I'll have half an hour before I catch the bus to Woodstock."

"You're a pal, Neil!" She smiled at him, showing dimples, and settled back in her seat.

A dark-haired guy in a black bomber jacket swished past them. Turning around, he came up to them again, nodded sternly at Maddie, and gave Neil a scornful once-over.

"So that *is* him!" Neil said. "You're way better off with me."

"I know, right?" she said. "How old are you anyway? Fifteen?"

Was she kidding? He smiled mysteriously and said nothing.

They chatted happily until they reached Edmundston where her brother was, in fact, waiting.

The drive to Woodstock passed quickly enough, but by the time Neil got off the bus from his last leg to Saint John, he was stiff and sore and totally exhausted. He was never getting on a bus again.

chapter 10

THE SAINT JOHN BUS STATION HAD a faint smell of the sea, but was as cold and scruffy as the rest. Neil had no idea where to go from there. Exhausted and hungry, he bought himself a hot chocolate and slumped on a bench to think.

A girl at a phone booth near him slammed the phone down and stomped off. A directory swayed on its chain beneath the shelf. Neil jumped up. That was how he could find his grandfather.

It was just the business directory, but he located the stable eventually, under the heading *Riding Academies*. It was called MacLeod's Equestrian Centre, and was located somewhere with the strange name of Quispamsis. An area map on the wall showed that it wasn't too far from Saint John.

Maybe he should phone his grandfather from here? His cellphone was dead, so he picked up the heavy, black receiver and began slowly dialling the numbers. Then he stopped. It would be better, he decided, replacing the receiver, more of a surprise, if he just turned up.

He put on his rain slicker for some protection from the cold wind and the threat of rain, and was soon standing at the side of the busy road out of Saint John, sticking out his thumb and shivering as he prepared to wait.

Car after car whizzed by, many of them expensive-looking. A Lexus hovered for a moment but sped up again, the driver presumably not liking the look of him. Finally a big old truck, labelled *Melanson Movers,* slowed and pulled up.

"Where you going, buddy?" the driver asked in a strong French accent, lowering the window as Neil came panting up.

"Um, somewhere near Quispamsis, I think."

"You *think*?" The man raised his eyebrows. "Any other clue?"

Neil put his backpack down. "Well, it's a riding stable, and the phone book said Quispamsis."

The truck driver grinned. "You're in luck, man! I'm going to Hamilton, but I'm in no hurry. I can take the scenic route and swing by Quispamsis. We'll find this stable for sure. Hop in."

Neil gratefully threw his backpack in and climbed up into the high cab and onto the cracked seat, taking in the smell of tobacco, chewing gum, and pine air-freshener.

"I'm Jean-Paul," the man said with a grin.

"Hi. I'm Neil."

"Well, do up your seat belt, Neil, and let's go find this stable. Have a gum." He held out a packet of Chiclets, then put the truck in gear and merged noisily back into the traffic. "Won't take us more than half an hour to get to Quispamsis," he said.

"Thanks." What a stroke of luck! Neil could hardly believe he was nearly there. He pictured the smiling man in the photo with the lovely horse. His grandfather would be surprised all right, but he'd surely be pleased to see him.

LINDA I WILL LOVE YOU FOREVER.
The big black letters, painted on a wall of rock, swung into view as the truck took a curve on the road from Saint John. Neil turned to watch the words recede before huddling back into his hoodie.

What would it be like to make such a promise for the whole world to see, he thought, let alone Linda, whoever she was? Was it even possible to be so sure? He dropped his gaze to the truck floor, littered with gum wrappers and cigarette packets.

"You know somebody at that stable?" the truck driver said, making another stab at conversation.

"Yup. My grandfather."

"Your grandfather, eh?" He looked at Neil. "I got grandkids," he said proudly. "Two of 'em. A boy, three, and a little girl, one and a half." He took his wallet out of his shirt pocket and flipped it open at a photo of two fat little grinning faces.

"Nice," said Neil.

"Joy of my life." Jean-Paul put the wallet away. "Little monkeys, both of them. Your grandpa, he'll be looking forward to seeing you, for sure." He glanced across at Neil. "How come he didn't meet you?"

"Um, he doesn't know I'm coming," said Neil. "It's a surprise."

Jean-Paul gave him another sideways look.

Ignoring an uncomfortable feeling in his gut, Neil turned to look out the side window.

Jean-Paul leaned forward to turn up the radio, comb marks showing in his dark hair. A song filled the truck with whirling, pounding energy, making the plastic hula dancer on the dash jiggle madly beneath the Virgin Mary swaying from the mirror.

"Good stuff, eh?" Jean-Paul shouted. "You like rock?"

"Uh-huh." He suddenly felt very tired.

Jean-Paul lowered the volume and shifted to look at him. "Look, buddy, I give you a ride, you can at least talk to me. That's the deal. You need a lift, and I need company." He looked back at the road with a sigh. "It's a boring life you know, driving around in a truck all day, every day."

"Sorry, man," said Neil. "I'm just no good at conversation." He was dead beat and starving after his marathon journey.

Jean-Paul leaned forward to peer into his face as he turned the radio back up. "Don't worry about it, kid," he shouted over the sudden blast of music. "You don't have to talk if you don't want to."

Leaning his head against the rattling window, Neil watched the tidy bungalows slip by, the wide river over on the driver's side glinting under what was left of the pale sunset. He looked at his watch: five-thirty. They must be getting near. "What's the name of this river?" he shouted, trying to be sociable.

Jean-Paul turned down the music. "Oh, that's the Kennebccasis River," he said proudly. "It meets up with the Saint John River, *and* with the sea back in town." He looked at Neil. "You ever hear of the Reversing Falls?"

Neil shook his head.

"No? It's real famous. One of the wonders of the world. You stay 'round here, man, you gotta see that!"

The road now ran past big fancy white houses set back behind smooth wide lawns and surrounded by huge trees. Occasional glimpses of the river kept appearing in the distance. The ad in the phone book had said that the stable was just outside Quispamsis, which, as he'd seen on the map, was quite close to another place called Rothesay. They'd surely be there soon.

"That was Rothesay we just went through," Jean-Paul said, as if reading Neil's thoughts. "Where all the millionaires live." He rolled his eyes and grinned. He offered Neil another gum and popped one in his own mouth.

"Won't be long now," he said. "Quispamsis is coming up soon, and then we've got to find that stable you're aiming for. You got the street number?"

"Um..." Neil thought hard. He had seen the number in the phone book and had assumed he would remember it, but it had gone out of his head. I can't remember," he said. "I know it had an eight in it and a nine...sorry."

Jean-Paul grinned. "No problem. We'll find it. There won't be too many stables around there, I don't think." He laughed, then looked at Neil. "Piece of luck for you that I could take the slow road, eh?"

A short way past the little town of Quispamsis, they slowed down as Jean-Paul squinted up the road. "There's a notice up ahead," he said. "Says *MacLeod's Equestrian Centre*. That it?"

"Yeah, that's it!" Neil grabbed his backpack as the truck stopped opposite a wide metal gate.

He jumped down. "Thanks a lot, Jean-Paul," he said, looking back up. "It was nice talking to you."

Jean-Paul laughed. "My pleasure, man," he said. "You take care of yourself now."

chapter 11

NEIL SHUT THE GATE BEHIND HIM, then turned and looked around in the fading light at the place that could become his new home. Fenced fields spread out on each side of a driveway that led up to a white-frame bungalow with an old black truck parked in front. Beyond the bungalow, a large barn was joined to a low metal structure. Behind that, another field sloped up to a darkly wooded hillside. A faint smell of manure hung in the cold air, but Neil couldn't see any horses. Just a donkey, standing by itself at the far end of the field.

His eyes fixed on the bungalow, he pulled his rain slicker tighter against the biting wind, and walked up the long, hard-packed gravel driveway. Ken had looked really nice in the photo, he thought. Neil was sure his grandfather would greet him with a big smile and probably make him a hot meal: pork chops, maybe, or a steak, and apple crumble.

He jumped in fright as a small but fierce-looking brown and white dog raced down the driveway yapping like crazy, stopping a couple of yards in front of him and sure as heck not about to let him get any closer. Sasha had taught him how to greet a strange dog, so he offered it the back of his closed hand, but it stood its ground, barking even more furiously and showing scarily large fangs.

Then the door of the bungalow opened and a short, bowlegged figure appeared, silhouetted against the yellow light. Surely that wasn't a gun in his hands?

"What're you doing on my land?" the man bellowed, hitching up his jeans as he came down the steps. "Don't you know you're trespassing?"

He called the dog off and squinted down the driveway. "Who the hell are you?"

It really was a gun, Neil saw as the man came closer. This couldn't be his grandfather's stable. He must have come to the wrong place. Possibly to the house of a killer. He felt his knees go weak, but then he saw the big, sticking-out ears.

"I...I'm Neil," he stammered. "Your grandson, Neil!"

The man lowered the gun. "What the devil?" He stared at him. "Adam's kid? What are you doing here?"

"I've...left home," Neil said weakly, "and...and I thought I'd come here."

"Well you bloody well thought wrong! You can't come here! It's out of the question!" He glared at Neil.

Neil looked down at the dog, shivering in the cold wind. What was he going to do? Where could he go in the dark and the cold, in the middle of nowhere? He felt his chin begin to wobble.

His grandfather gave an angry sigh. "You'd better come in for now, I suppose," he said, "until we figure out how to send you back. I don't know where the hell we're going to put you, though."

Neil looked at the denim-jacketed back in front of him as Ken pushed open the door. It was hard to believe that this was the smiling man from Margaret's photos.

"You might as well meet Cheryl," Ken said as he turned off the boxy little TV set. He pointed to a tanned woman with long streaky dark-blond hair. "Cheryl, this is my grandson, apparently. Neil."

The woman stubbed out her cigarette, smiled, and held out her hand. "How ya doin,' kid?"

He began to feel a little bit better as they shook hands, the dog jumping up and wagging its short tail. This was terrible, but at least he hadn't been shot, and was out of the wind, and had somewhere to sleep.

"You carried this *all* the way?" Cheryl seemed to be amused as she hefted his backpack.

"I suppose you're hungry." Ken said, getting himself a beer from the fridge. "I've got a frozen dinner in there somewhere. That suit you?"

Neil nodded quickly. He'd never had a frozen dinner in his life, but whatever it was, he would have eaten it straight from the packet.

"Here, I'm popping it in the nuker for you," Cheryl said. "A Hungry Man Dinner. There's Coke in the fridge, and Cheesies in the cupboard to tide you over. C'mon, Keeper. See you guys tomorrow." She slung an old jean jacket over her plaid flannel shirt and went out the back door followed by the dog.

Neil and his grandfather looked at each other awkwardly in the silence.

"You might as well sit down." Ken pointed to a dilapidated armchair by the electric fire and banged a knife and fork down on the table.

Neil felt he'd done enough sitting for a lifetime, but sat obediently and looked around at the cracked, imitation wood floor and white Formica table with steel chairs. There was another, bigger armchair opposite him and a greasy-looking sofa under the window.

Ken brought his beer and sat across from him as they waited for the ping of the microwave.

"Where've you come from anyway?" he asked after taking a swig. "I heard years ago that Adam was in Vancouver. Don't tell me you've come all the way from there?"

"No, we've just come to live in Ottawa to be near Margaret. My mother's just had an accident. She's still in hospital but she's going to be all right."

"Big help you're being then!" Ken frowned. "Did they know you were coming here?"

"No," said Neil, turning away from Ken's glare. "I just ran away."

"So they have no idea where you are? What the hell were you thinking, boy? They must be going nuts with worry!" He pointed to the phone on the wall beside the fridge. "Give Margaret a call! Right now!"

Neil saw again the torn-up album, the scraps of photographs scattered on the carpet. He felt terrible. Margaret had been nothing but nice to him, and this was how he'd repaid her. He put his head in his hands and stared at the coating of brown and white dog hairs on the smelly matted rug at his feet. If only he could just eat and go straight to bed.

"Go on!" Ken said. "Phone!

Neil punched the numbers with shaking fingers and heard the familiar ring.

Margaret picked up right away. "Oh Neil! Thank God! We've been looking everywhere for you, going out of our minds with worry! Where on earth are you?"

"I'm at my grandfather's," he said.

"You're *what?*"

His grandfather took the plastic dish out of the microwave and put it straight on the table.

"You're with *Ken*?" Her voice was almost a squeak.

More silence, while Neil stared at a crack in the wall.

"But how in the world did you get there, Neil?"

"By bus."

"Good grief!" There was another pause. "Well, I suppose you'd better stay there until we decide how to get you back."

Miserably, he twiddled the phone cord. "I'm really sorry, Margaret," he said. "About all the mess...."

"The mess you made is the least of it," she said. "I understand you were terribly shocked. You weren't supposed to see those photographs. But we've been horribly stressed with worry, Neil. So much so, your mom has had to delay coming out of hospital."

He closed his eyes. "But she's going to be okay?"

"I think so. No thanks to you! How could you, Neil?" she said, her voice shaking. There was another pause. "What are we going to do about you? You can't stay with Ken! He's totally unsuitable, and anyway he wouldn't want you there. Put him on the phone!"

Neil held the phone out to a reluctant Ken, who pointed silently at the dinner waiting on the table.

In spite of everything, Neil gobbled up his surprisingly tasty dinner as his grandparents argued, until he heard Ken shout, "Well, I sure don't want him! You'd better take him, Margaret. And you can tell that...*thing*, it's no wonder the kid ran away. Who wouldn't?" He slammed the phone down and glared at Neil before swigging his beer.

Neil pushed the last of his dinner away. What if Sasha heard what Ken had just said? He felt sick and guilty, and ashamed of his grandfather.

***

"Margaret's pretty mad at you," Ken said, sounding a bit less angry as they sat later by the fire. "But she blames herself for letting that happen with the photographs." He looked away with a shrug, wiping his mouth after another go at his beer. "And, of course, the bottom line is that she blames me for deserting the sinking ship all that time ago." He sighed and stretched out his legs, showing a hole in the toe of his thick gray work sock. "But what are you gonna do, eh? At the end of the day, when all's said and done, I'm just a run-of-the-mill kind of guy. I don't buy into that stuff."

Neil looked at the scruffy figure in front of him and screwed up his courage. He had to ask. "Is my...is Sasha really doing okay?"

"Yes. I gather he, er, I mean"—Ken bared his uneven teeth—"Sasha's going to be fine. Margaret told me to tell you that; and she said you should know that Sasha—" he almost spat out the name—"was planning to tell you everything the night of the accident, but you blew up and ran off before she had a chance. Margaret says Sasha feels terrible. Feels she's completely to blame for everything, apparently. And you know, I gotta say I would agree with that."

Ken scratched his stubbly cheek and looked away. "To tell you the truth, I've always blamed Adam for the whole mess. At the end of the day, I reckon the buck stops with him. I know Margaret has always said it wasn't Adam's fault, and that he couldn't help it if that was the hand he'd been dealt. Just between you and me, I just don't see why he had to screw up everybody else's life instead of keeping it to himself, the way other people of his sort do."

To his embarrassment, Neil felt tears rising. This was so unfair. Ken was a horrible father.

Ken jerked his head back, frowning. "I shouldn't be talking to you like this, for Christ's sake! You're just a kid. How old are you anyway? Thirteen? Fourteen?"

"Thirteen," said Neil, quietly.

They sat in silence for a while. Neil's head ached and he felt dizzy. He hung his head and clasped his hands between his knees. If he hadn't run off like that and turned off his cellphone, the accident would never have happened and he wouldn't be sitting here with a grandfather who didn't even want him.

Then, with a hard pain in his chest, he remembered why he'd run away in the first place.

Ken stood up. "You look done in. You need to hit the hay. You can stay here for tonight anyway, and we'll decide what to do with you tomorrow."

chapter 12

NEIL WOKE IN THE SMALL, BARE room to the smell of bacon frying and the sound of chatter from the radio or TV. It was broad daylight. His watch said nine-fifteen. Despite everything, he'd slept in this narrow iron bed for well over twelve hours.

He rubbed his eyes and sat up. So, that was his grandfather. Well, he'd just have to turn to Plan B: find Jessica, and see if he could live with her. Which was probably the best plan anyway.

The bathroom was small and a bit grungy, but not too bad. In the shower stall he found, to his surprise, a bottle of purple, flower-scented body wash. He saw a woman's deodorant on a shelf in the medicine cabinet and found a shiny red hair-dryer stashed in the cupboard under the wash basin. This stuff obviously wasn't Ken's. Did that mean that Cheryl normally lived here?

He rubbed steam off the window pane with the thin grayish towel and looked out onto the back field. There were the horses! Six of them, all facing the same way, heads down, cropping the short yellow grass. He wondered as he studied them if that was enough for a stable.

They were all different colours, and not smooth and shining in the sun like you might expect. They were fuzzy-looking, although the dark brown one with the long blond mane and tail, just like the horse in the photo, was shinier than the others. The black horse was the biggest by far. The smallest and the shaggiest was a Shetland pony, the same colour as the crabapples still hanging on the tree beside the bathroom window.

At the other end of the paddock, the donkey watched a man in the next field over. Neil felt a rush of sympathy for the donkey. Had he been cast out from the herd because he was different, he wondered, or did he just prefer to be alone?

He turned to get dressed but stopped, staring in dismay at the clean clothes, taken from his backpack and placed on the chair.

"Where's my other jeans?" he asked, striding fully dressed into the kitchen.

"And top of the morning to you, too." Ken moved stiffly about the kitchen, keenly watched by the dog, Keeper. He seemed to be in a much better mood. He shovelled two fried eggs, dripping with fat, onto an already loaded plate. "Here's your breakfast. Best meal of the day, I always say." He plonked the plate down on the table. "Your jeans are in the wash, so you'll be clean for your journey back. Don't worry. I checked the pockets first."

To his relief, Neil saw the photograph of Jessica safe and dry on the counter, and sat down to eat.

There was bacon on his plate—four strips of it, not just a garnish—two fat, brown, glistening sausages; two eggs, crisply frilled at the edges and speckled with dark flecks; a pile of delicious little potato puff things. There were even baked beans. Sasha never made him breakfasts like this, he thought. Homemade granola was about as exciting as it got. She never gave him coffee either, but here was Ken, placing a big steaming mug of it in front of him.

"What do you know about this girl?" Ken said, picking up the photo of Jessica.

Swallowing hard, Neil leaned back in the chair, his eyes fixed on the photo. Maybe this was his chance to find out more about Jessica and where to find her. "I know that she's my real mother," he said, his mouth dry. "And I'd like to have that back, please."

Frowning, Ken silently handed him the creased photo.

"I'm going to find her, and maybe live with her," said Neil, refolding the photo and putting it back in his pocket. He took a long drink of coffee and settled down to his breakfast. "Do you have any idea where she might be?"

"I need to talk to you before we phone the bus station," Ken said after a moment.

Neil mopped up the remains of his meal with a piece of buttered toast and washed it down with a last, extra-sweet gulp of coffee as Ken sat down beside him. The dog's claws clicked on the vinyl floor as he pushed his way in to sit between them.

"I'm sorry to have to tell you this, Neil." Ken scratched his head and pointed his chin across the room. "I thought you would know, but this girl Jessica...well, I'm afraid she died."

Neil froze, feeling only the pressure of the dog against his leg.

Ken cleared his throat. "She passed soon after she handed you over to Adam. She had, um...she had a"—he raised his eyebrows to look at Neil and then quickly away—"she had a drug problem."

A sudden strange and horrible noise came from outside. Neil jumped up in fright.

"Calm down! That's just the donkey," Ken said. He jerked his chin up and cleared his throat. "Anyway, that was why she gave you to Adam. At least that's what I heard." He glanced back at Neil. "For your sake, you understand. Because she knew she wouldn't make it."

As Neil sat down, Keeper licked his hand with a warm tongue.

"I gather from Margaret that he, or I suppose I should say she," Ken pulled a sour face,

"Sasha, that is, came back into the picture after that. She's looked after you ever since."

Neil's breakfast had become a cold, heavy lump in his stomach. Scraping back his chair, he stumbled to the bathroom.

chapter 13

NEIL PUT BOTH HANDS ON TOP OF the fence post and rested his forehead on them, tears of grief and anger in his eyes. Jessica, his real mother, was dead. She had been dead all along. And before she died, she had given him away. She looked so lovely in the photo. Neil was sure he could remember her. He had set his heart on finding her and looking after her. He clutched the post and cried for his lost mother, and for his lost hopes.

Drying his tears, he thought about his situation. What could he do now? Ken sure didn't want him, and any hope of finding Jessica had vanished. He looked across the paddock to the great silver river sliding silently by in the distance. There was no way he could go back to his so-called mother after what he'd discovered, but where *could* he go? He kicked the post, sending a shudder down the fence and getting an evil sideways look from the red pony.

"Hey, Neil!" Cheryl shouted from the barn door. "Wanna give me a hand? I could use some help."

Neil wiped his eyes and walked over. A distraction, maybe that's what he needed.

The barn was warm and shadowy and sweet smelling. Cheryl looked up from brushing out a stall. "Our stable-boy, Stephane, quit a couple of days ago," she said, "and I gotta do everything, since Ken's all seized-up these days." She pointed to a well worn pair of leather boots in the corner. "Those belonged to Stephane. Why don't you throw them on and help me muck out? No point spoiling them fancy runners."

As they worked, Cheryl explained the art of mucking out. "The main thing," she said, using the pitchfork to sift out lumps of manure, "is to take out as much of this stuff and wet bedding as you can without wasting any good stuff, and put in just enough fresh straw or shavings to make it comfortable."

Cheryl didn't seem to mind that he didn't feel like talking. They worked together until all the stalls were clean and ready and the hay nets were filled.

"Good stuff!" she said as he came back from taking the last load out to the manure pile. "Thanks. Now, are you up to helping me bring in a couple of horses? There's someone coming for a trail ride later, and a girl wanting a lesson."

Neil nodded and followed her. If he was here, he might as well be useful.

She handed him a lead-shank. "See if you can fetch Honey, that's the gold-coloured one nearest us. Just walk up to her, all matter-of-fact, and fasten this clip onto the halter ring under her chin. I'll go get Dude."

"Dude?" He looked at her in surprise. "But isn't he super old? My grandma said she used to ride a horse named Dude, and I saw one here this morning, just like the horse in her photo."

Cheryl laughed. "That was Old Dude, Ken's favourite Rocky Mountain horse from long ago. This one is Little Dude, Old Dude's grandson."

Three horses ambled up: the two they wanted, plus the big black one. "This one's Onyx," Cheryl said, giving the black horse a smack on his big behind to move him out of the way. "He's checking to see if there's any short-feed going. He's a greedy old guy and likes to have his own way." They watched Onyx slope off. "Now, put the lead-shank on Honey while I get Dude."

Small, pretty Honey stood perfectly still while Neil clipped the lead on her halter, and waited quietly beside him until Cheryl came up with Dude.

"What are the others called?" he asked after they had brought in the two horses.

Cheryl led him to the barn door. "That one's Pinto," she said, pointing to a large black and white pony in the paddock. "And that brown and white one next to him is his sidekick, Nino. They always hang out together, just like Onyx and Honey."

"And who's that?" He pointed at the little red pony.

She laughed. "That's Mackie. The little devil. He's an escape artist. You always have to be super careful to check the gate fastenings and keep the fences in good shape, or he's off looking for greener pastures. He's cute, but he's as mean as they come, so watch out."

He looked over to the other end of the field where the donkey stood, staring into space. "What's the donkey called?"

"Olive used to call him Benjamin," she said. "She liked him a lot, but now he's just The Donkey."

"Who's Olive?"

"You don't know? She was Ken's wife. She died a couple of years ago. Cancer."

"Oh, I see." He frowned, thinking of Margaret. "What was she like?"

"Real nice. She was sick for a long time though. In and out of hospital. Stayed there in the end." She shook herself and looked at Neil. "Wanna see how to groom a horse?

Did he ever. "Sure!" he said, watching eagerly as she fetched Dude and clipped him to the posts on each side of the aisle.

"First thing to learn about handling a horse," she said, "is how not to get kicked if you're in back of him. You either stand close to the horse's rump, like this," she demonstrated, "coming up from the side and putting your hand on him first, to let him know you're there, or you make sure to keep far enough away to escape being kicked if he's startled—or mean like Mackie.

Let's see you come up to the back end of Dude. Remember what I said, now!"

He approached Dude, doing as she said.

"Good stuff! Now for the grooming. You start with cleaning out their hooves," she said. "That's the hardest bit, and a big strain on the back until you get used to it. Let's put Honey behind Dude, and you can watch me and make a start with her."

After she'd fetched Honey, she said, "The thing is to prop the hoof up on your knee like this." Her back to him, she slid her hand down Dude's near-front leg and pulled the foot up to rest on her bent knee. "And get the muck out with the hoof-pick, always working away from the sensitive bulge in the middle, like this. See?" She picked a clump of dried earth and a small stone out of Dude's hoof. "See if you can do that with Honey's front foot."

It was all Neil could do to get the hoof in position, but he did manage to dislodge a chunk of hard mud before he had to stand up and let Cheryl take over. He watched, amazed at how cooperatively Dude was lifting each hoof in what seemed like the agreed-upon order, standing still on three legs while Cheryl poked and scraped. He noticed, too, how gently she set each hoof down when she'd finished.

Next, she showed him how to pick out burs and untangle and brush the mane and tail; how to work the round curry comb in circles to loosen the mud and dried sweat on the horse's hide before flicking out the dirt with the stiff brush, not forgetting to keep cleaning the brush with the curry comb.

After that, she said, you went over the horse again with the softer body brush, shining it up all over, switching to an even softer brush for the horse's bony face, where you should never use a rough one. "That's the bit they like best," she said, and he could see for himself how totally relaxed Dude became under the smooth brush, his head low and his eyes soft.

"Here," she said, "you finish Dude off with the body brush while I get going on Honey."

His worries forgotten temporarily, Neil worked away, smoothing and polishing, taking in the good smell of the horse's hide and watching Dude's nut-coloured coat become glossy under the brush. He looked up to see Cheryl watching him.

"You got a real good way with animals," she said. After they put the horses away, she gave his shoulder a playful punch. "I guess you're the man in charge for a bit now, kid, while me and Ken nip in to Quispamsis to pick up some sweet feed before the riders come."

Neil sat on a bale of hay and watched Cheryl walk off. Alone in the barn, the warm, friendly feeling slowly sinking away, he tried again to decide what he should do.

It was clear that Ken meant to send him back as soon as possible, but he was not going back there. Ever. Biting his lip, he hung his head.

Sasha had lied to him his whole life. Thanks to her, his entire life was a fake. All his memories of her were mistaken, just like his stupid search for his non-existent father. He resolved again to wipe out all thoughts of her. Of Margaret. Of Jessica. He needed to forget Courtenay too, he thought, since there was no way he could go back and make up with her. Other people turned their backs on bad stuff and made a new life for themselves, he thought. If Ken could do it, why couldn't he?

He heard whinnying from the paddock but figured it must be normal. But the frantic neigh that came a few minutes later was definitely not. He jumped up and ran out of the barn and saw, to his horror, the black horse, Onyx, grazing in the open field on the other side of the road, which was already getting busy with the late-morning traffic. Honey was trotting, head high along the fenceline, neighing and looking for a way to join her pal.

He had to do something. And he had to do it now.

He ran down, shooed Honey away, and straightened the fence post as well as he could. Then he rushed back to the barn, grabbed a lead-shank and, after a moment's thought, quickly shovelled some sweet feed into a bucket.

Once across the road, he shook the bucket noisily and walked carefully up to Onyx, trying hard to send out calm, confident vibes like Cheryl.

The big horse kept shifting away from him, snatching at the long dry grass until the sound and smell became too much for him. He ambled up, snorting and shaking his ears, and stuck his head in the bucket. Neil immediately put his hand in to feel for the metal loop in the halter. Holding his breath, his fingers shaking, he managed to clip on the lead-shank.

He had met the first challenge successfully. Now he had to get Onyx back across the road. He picked up the bucket and led the horse to the roadside. Too hooked on the sweet feed to be bothered by traffic, Onyx calmly rootled away as cars whizzed by. Even when a school bus went past, the kids all sticking their heads out and yelling, Onyx pulled out his nose for just one scary moment before getting back to the unexpected feast.

As soon as there was a big enough gap in the traffic, Neil led Onyx, still guzzling, across the road and through the gate. He took him up the driveway and right into his stall. Then he fetched and stabled all the others just to make sure they were safe. As he shut the last bolt, he realized that he was shaking.

***

When Ken and Cheryl returned, Neil told them what had happened. He could tell by the look they exchanged that they were impressed with his quick thinking. After they fixed the fence and let the horses back out, the three of them sat around the kitchen table, having sandwiches.

"If it wasn't for you, Neil," Ken said, "both of those horses could have been killed. The other horses could have got out too." He shuddered. "Could have been a lot worse, even. Someone could have been hurt or killed, and that would have been curtains for this place. And for me."

Cheryl agreed. "It was real smart of you to take the sweet feed, Neil," she said. "I couldn't have done better myself." She turned to Ken. "You know, Ken, in just a few hours, this kid has proven himself a much better stable hand than Stephane ever was." She looked hard at him. "Your arthritis is pretty bad just now, and I'm struggling with doing all the work myself. Couldn't we keep Neil around for a few days, until we can find more help?"

Ken thought for a moment and then straightened his shoulders with a grunt. "I guess a week or so wouldn't hurt," he said. "We sure could do with a hand." He eased himself out of his chair. "I can't pay you, but while you're here, Neil, just to show my appreciation, I'll give you a few riding lessons, if you want."

Neil grinned at his grandfather. This was way better than money, he thought. This was exactly what he wanted: to learn how to ride a horse.

chapter 14

"YOU OBVIOUSLY TAKE AFTER ME," KEN said after Neil's first go in the ring on easygoing old Piper. "You're a born rider, with a naturally good seat and perfect balance." He thought for a bit. "In fact," he said, "since you're so promising, let's see how you do on Dude."

Neil was thrilled. He'd dreamed of riding that lovely horse.

"You'll have to take care," Ken warned. "Dude's a whole different kettle of fish. He's always hot to trot, so you'll need to go easy on the signals. And keep a steady hand on the reins, or he'll tear away on you. I'll show you about that in the next lesson. Just do what I say for now, and you'll be all right."

Neil felt the horse's energy and power as soon as he sat on Dude. And the smooth running-walk the breed was famous for felt like floating on air after Piper's jolting trot. Dude obeyed every signal, stopping and starting, and turning, and changing from a walk to a trot. Who knew riding a horse was so easy?

After the lesson, Ken leaned against the door-post. "I talked to your grandmother again last night," he said. "They don't want you doing that marathon bus trip again, and the doctor says your, er, you know, Sasha, should wait a few more days before travelling. They want you to stay a bit longer, and then someone will fly down in a few days to get you."

Neil looked down, kicking at a stick.

"Earth to Neil!" Ken said, knocking at the doorpost.

"I can't go back!" Neil said. "You don't know what it'll be like for me living with that..." he looked away and then straight back at Ken, "that *freak*."

Neil felt a hot wave of shame run over him. He felt terrible every time Ken called Sasha names, and now that he'd done it himself, he felt sick. But he had to stop Ken sending him back, and this seemed like the only way to do it. He looked hard at his grandfather. "Would *you* want to live like that?"

Ken looked away, scratching his chin.

"Can't I stay here, Ken?" he pleaded. "I love it here. I love working with the horses and riding and everything! And I like being with you and Cheryl. Please, Ken, let me stay!"

Ken straightened himself. "I can't possibly be responsible for you full-time, Neil," he said. "But you're welcome to stay until they come for you, of course, and you can always come back for a visit." Walking slowly, Ken left the barn.

***

The next day, while Cheryl and Neil were getting ready to go on Neil's first trail ride, Ken came out to the barn with a warning. "Gord told me just now that there's illegal hunting happening on his property," he said to Cheryl, referring to a neighbour. "Be sure to wear something bright and use white saddle blankets just in case. Some of those hunters wouldn't know a deer from a donkey."

Wow, this was living dangerously, Neil thought excitedly as they followed Ken's instructions—even down to his wearing Ken's red barn jacket.

First, they walked and then trotted the horses, one behind the other, along the path. The scent of crushed pine needles was fresh on the cold air. There was no snow yet, but the horses' breath plumed white from their nostrils. The woods were silent, apart from the soft thud of hooves, the creak and jingle of saddles and bits, and the occasional little outburst from a chickadee.

Dude was already tossing his head impatiently when Cheryl gave the signal to speed up. Trees and rocks flew by as they tore along the hard-packed ground. *I can totally do this*, Neil thought, leaning forward in the saddle. *I could run forever!*

Ahead of him Onyx skittered and stopped dead, his ears pointing forward. Neil managed to halt Dude and stay on. He looked up to see a man standing on the path in front of them.

Small and thin, the man had long, graying black hair and wore an old leather jacket over faded jeans tucked into moccasin-type boots. His blue eyes were fixed on Neil in what looked like horror.

"*C'est correct, Luc*! It's okay!" Cheryl called out. "It's just Neil, Ken's grandson. He's staying with us for a bit."

Put off by the man's panicky stare, Neil looked down and patted Dude's neck. When he raised his head a couple of seconds later, the man was gone. There'd been no crackle of twigs or rustle of branches, nor could the man be seen slipping through the trees in any direction. He had simply disappeared into the forest.

"That was Luc," Cheryl said, looking back at Neil as they took up their ride again at a walk. "He's an old friend of mine. He's used to me and Honey's owner, Margot, and a few other people riding out here, but total strangers spook him. Luc lives wild, and he keeps away from people. Sort of like a hermit."

"Why?" Neil asked, leaning forward to hear her better. The man had been still and silent, like an animal scenting danger, and then suddenly invisible, like a ghost. "What's wrong with him?"

"Oh, he's totally messed up, poor guy, but he's harmless. I'll tell you about him later."

They trotted along until they reached the rock that marked the turning point, then turned the horses to go home. As they walked back, Cheryl returned to the subject of Luc, "His story's real bad. The poor guy can't hardly deal with people at all. Me, Kevin at the store, and Gord, the farmer up the road, we're just about the only ones he talks to. C'mon, let's have a short canter." At that, she took off; Neil followed.

"But where does he live?" asked Neil, as they slowed down to a walk. "What about food? And shelter?"

"He lives in a log cabin way up in the woods," Cheryl replied. "Gord owns nearly all the land 'round here and he lets Luc have the cabin in exchange for work. He has a garden, and he hunts a bit and gathers stuff, and if he needs anything else he writes a list and hands it in at the store to pick up later. People look out for him. He gets by okay."

"But does he have any friends? Does anyone ever go to see him?"

"Like I said, he keeps away from people."

"But what if he gets sick? Who'd look after him then?"

"There's a few of us, like me and Kevin and Gord, who keep an eye on him. Anyways, he's tough as old boots." She turned on Neil. "What's it to you anyways? I thought you was so wrapped up in your own misery, you got no time for anyone else's problems."

"What?" Neil felt his face flush.

"From what I hear, everybody's looking out for you. Sasha, who's been waiting on you, hand and foot, your whole life; your grandma, phoning every blessed night to ask how you are. Ken tells me there's even a girl worrying about you, back in Ottawa. Everyone's bending over backwards to make sure poor Neil's okay."

She stopped talking as they neared the barn. When they had finished with the horses, Cheryl pointed her crop at some bales left ready on the floor for the morning. "Just sit yourself there, pal, and I'll tell you about some real problems."

Stalks of straw pricked through Neil's jeans as he sat down. The barn cat crept out from between the bales, hissed, and slunk away.

He sat, mesmerized, as the horses pulled hay out of the nets, munching noisily. Onyx neighed and Honey nickered back as Cheryl walked a few yards down the concrete aisle, turned on her heel, and strode back.

"Long story short..." she stood in front of him, feet apart, fists on hips. Taking a deep breath, she stared at him, eyes wide, before she spoke: "Long story short, Luc's mom went crazy and murdered his dad. They were fighting, and she grabbed the rifle off the wall and shot him dead."

A thump and a squeal came from the paint ponies' double stall. Neil hung his head, squeezing his eyes tight shut.

"Oh yes, you heard me." Cheryl's hoarse voice went on, "Luc was ten at the time, and he seen the whole thing."

Neil stared at her in horror. This was the most terrible thing he had heard in his whole life! He shivered and licked his dry lips.

"What happened to Luc then?" he managed to whisper.

"Oh, his grandma took him in, of course. That's what grandmas are for, right?" She looked across at him. "Anyways, after that, he wouldn't say nothing. Not a word. Wouldn't go to school either. And if anyone yelled or there was a big noise, he'd run off and hide, for days sometimes."

"But where did he run to?"

"Into the forest. I guess he felt safe there, poor guy. After his grandma passed, when he wasn't much older than you, he moved into the old cabin."

Neil stared at her. "You mean, he was only my age and he went to live by himself in a cabin deep in the woods?" The idea was worrying, but at the same time very cool. He had so many questions. "Was it okay to live in?" he asked. "Not all gross, with mice and birds and stuff in it?"

Cheryl nodded. "It took him months to put it straight, and he needed lots of help of course, like with fixing the roof and the wood stove and stuff, but in the end, he got it done."

"Who helped him?"

"There were some people around, willing to give him a hand," she said. "His life is pretty basic, but he says he's got all he needs."

Neil watched a sparrow fly down the length of the barn and out through a hole in the back window. "He can talk, then?"

"Sure he can. He won't if he can help it, but he can if he has to. He talked his way out of being put in the loony bin, anyways."

"But is he always alone?" Neil asked again. "Doesn't anyone ever go to see him?"

Cheryl shrugged. "That's Luc. He lives his life, such as it is. That's all any of us can do." She flung on her jacket and turned away without looking at him. He got up to watch her cycle down to the road on her rusty, lime-green mountain bike, Keeper running behind her.

chapter 15

*T*HAT EVENING, OVER MAC AND cheese, Neil thought about how Cheryl had seemed a bit mad at him before in the barn. Had he turned her life upside down by coming here? He braced himself to ask Ken: "Was Cheryl living here before I came?"

Ken looked up, an orange forkful halfway to his mouth. "Why do you ask?"

"Well, I'm just saying, if she moved out because of me, I wouldn't mind if she came back.

I mean, she was here first. I mean, if she was here at all." He felt himself blush and bent over his plate, shovelling in the last mouthful.

"Oh, Cheryl comes and goes." Ken swabbed his plate with a piece of white bread. "I wouldn't worry your head about it."

When the phone rang at nine o'clock, its usual time, Neil grabbed his Coke and retreated to his bedroom, shutting the door firmly. The last thing he wanted was to hear Ken and Margaret quarrelling over him, but it was no use. Ken's shouting carried through the walls.

"You're going to have to take him, Margaret," Ken yelled. "I already told you, I'm sure as hell not sending him home to live with that—you know exactly what I mean. It's not right!"

Neil heard Ken open the fridge door and grab another beer as he listened to Margaret's response.

"Fine," said Ken. "See if I care." The phone slammed down.

Neil sat on his bed, wondering with a sick feeling if Margaret would relay Ken's ugly words to Sasha.

Trying to get his mind off all that, he grabbed his sketchbook and looked through the few drawings he'd managed to make since he'd arrived.

There was quite a good sketch of Dude in his stall, turning his head to look at him. And one of Keeper with a ball in his mouth, but one leg was all wrong. He'd managed to catch the mean look in Mackie's eye, and, although the proportions were off, he'd captured the cat's flattened ears and intense stare.

He put down the sketchbook. If Keeper were around, he could try another sketch of him, but he'd gone home with Cheryl. Anyway, the light was bad and there was no way he could concentrate.

Hearing Ken go into the bathroom, Neil got into his coat and sneakers and slipped out the back door. Although it was quite late, he could easily make out the hulk of the barn and the dark mass of the forest behind, and even the fence posts and lines.

Was the moon shining? He looked up and saw the stars as he'd never seen them before. The sky was filled with them, big ones and small ones, streaks and clusters, and one huge long mass which he thought must be the Milky Way. He felt weird and very small. If the whole world was just a tiny dot like that, what was he?

The horses nickered softly as he came into the barn. He felt the warmth and inhaled the sweet, musky smell of horses and hay as they munched and shifted in the dark. Dude turned his head to snuffle at him as Neil slipped into the stall.

Leaning against Dude's flank and stroking his silky neck, he thought again about Luc, whose mother really *had* killed his father, literally. There was no comparison between Luc's story and his, he knew. He had never had to witness a horrible scene like the one Luc had lived through.

He buried his face in Dude's thick mane, and tried to force himself to think of something else—the excitement of racing through the forest on Dude, the fun of playing ball with Keeper, or the comfort of grooming the donkey—but there was no peaceful place in his mind where he could hide.

Giving Dude a last pat, Neil left the stall and went to check on the others, all quiet and contented—even Mackie, who surprised him with a little *harrumph* of welcome.

There was no getting away from what Luc had been through, Neil thought as he walked in the starlight back to the bungalow. He slipped in through the back door and tiptoed past Ken, who was fast asleep on the sofa; he looked old, his head tipped back and his mouth open.

Neil thought about what Cheryl had said, about how easy he had it. She was right, he realized. He had it better than Courtenay, for sure, whose parents didn't seem to care about her nearly as much as Sasha cared about him.

He remembered Courtenay's shocked face when he'd shouted at her. He felt bad about her, and he missed her company. Cheryl said that a girl back home was worrying about him, but she must have got it wrong. Courtenay probably hated him. Or worse: she'd completely forgotten about him.

He tried to stop thinking, only to have Luc's story rise again in his mind in all its horror: the noise, the blood and gore, all happening right in front of the boy's eyes. How could any little kid get over that?

He remembered the way Luc had vanished into the forest and wondered where his cabin was. As he crawled into bed, exhausted, he tried to imagine what the cabin would be like.

Neil fell quickly into a deep sleep, dreaming first of Courtenay, walking backwards away from him with a reproachful look. And then of Sasha, stretched out on a hospital bed. She was dead, the ginger-haired nurse and stern doctor were telling him, their eyes hard emerald green and stony black. Dead, because of him. This morphed into a dream of Luc appearing and disappearing through the trees, his eyes fixed on Neil's. A glint of silver: Luc had a rifle and was aiming at him.

Neil woke up sweating, his heart thumping, still seeing the barrel levelled at his head.

***

In the morning, Neil was still shaken. He looked for Ken and was surprised to find him preparing to leave.

"I'm shutting the place down for the day," Ken said. "It's too cold for lessons or trail rides. Olive's sister and her husband, up in Hampton, are having some kind of an anniversary party. I figured I'd make an appearance. Cheryl's taking the day off, so you're on your own for a few hours."

He was torn: it was pretty neat that he'd have the place all to himself. But that dream was still nagging at him. "Cool," he said, shrugging his shoulders.

"I can't say what time I'll be back," Ken said as he got into the truck, "but there's leftover *tourtière* in the fridge for supper, and a can of baked beans in the cupboard. See you later."

Neil stood, watching him drive away. Maybe being left in charge wouldn't be so bad.

chapter 16

NEIL SAT ON THE MOUNTING BLOCK by the gate. He propped his sketchpad on his knee, and began making some quick drawings of the horses. First, Mackie, a chunky little mess, his big dark eyes the only important feature. Then muscular Onyx, with his big hairy feet, followed by compact, elegant little Honey. He wished he had his paints to capture the rich deep gold of her coat and the striking contrast between Dude's light blond mane and tail and walnut-coloured coat. The donkey was too far off to draw, and anyway, his fingers had gotten too stiff and cold to work.

He went to the barn to see what needed doing. Just about everything, it turned out. He got down to it. He mucked out the stalls, swept the aisle, and arranged the saddles on the proper racks in the tack-room, with the bridles hanging below. He even fed the grateful cat some leftover sardines. He really was a good stable hand, he thought, looking around. They needed him.

For the first time since he'd arrived here, he realized, he was truly alone. He didn't even have a dog to keep him company, since Keeper was with Cheryl. It would be nice to have a dog of his own. Keeper was always up for a romp or a chase, or a game of fetch. They had a dog once in Vancouver, Neil dimly remembered, when he was very small: a Westie called Babe, but she'd got run over, and Sasha'd said she'd never put herself through that again. One day, Neil thought, he'd get a dog for himself.

As he stood there, Neil became aware of the cold creeping through his layers of clothing and decided that Dude, who didn't have as thick a winter coat as the others, should have his blanket on.

After fetching Dude and tying him up to the hitching post in the barn, Neil went to grab the quilted blanket from the tack room. He pulled the heavy bundle off the high shelf, almost knocking Dude's saddle from its rack. As he straightened it, he heard an iron-shod hoof strike the cement floor. He glanced around. Full dark eyes shining and nostrils flaring, Dude was ready and willing for action.

Neil looked at his watch. It was only twenty past two. There were at least a couple of hours before it would start to get dark. Thinking hard, he replaced the folded blanket, bringing it neatly in line with the others.

Ken had banned any unsupervised riding, but surely there'd be no problem with taking Dude into the ring, just to put him through his paces, or maybe even a quick run in the paddock? Neil considered this. After all the practice he'd had and the ability he'd shown, especially on the day he'd saved Onyx, he figured he'd earned it.

He turned to look through the small, cob-webby window at the dark forest beyond. He could even, he supposed, his stomach tightening, take Dude out on a little trail ride. There would be no harm in it. Anyway, who would know?

He remembered Ken's warning about hunters and swapped Dude's brown saddle-blanket for a big white one. He then put Ken's red barn jacket on over his hoodie. All right, he thought, I should be safe enough now.

He warmed Dude up, as Ken always insisted, first walking then trotting him around the upper paddock a couple of times before cantering up to the start of the trail.

Cheryl had shown him how to open and close the gate from horseback, but it was a tricky business. Since the other horses were safely shut in the lower paddock and he'd only be gone for a short time, he left the gate open for his return.

He zipped up the jacket and fastened his helmet. Then he sat up straight, pushed his heels down, and urged Dude into the running-walk.

For a couple of minutes they clipped along the hard, well-beaten track, until he couldn't resist letting Dude speed up, daringly, into a full gallop. Neil's eyes watered and his fingers, in their thin riding gloves, were already stiff with cold, but he laughed out loud at the incredible thrill.

When he finally tried reining Dude in, the way he'd practiced with Ken in the paddock, he found there was no holding the horse back.

He knew he couldn't panic and hung in, weight still forward, elbows tight, his hands creeping up the reins and alternately pulling back and letting go, the way Ken had demonstrated. He couldn't find a convenient clearing where he could turn, so the whole thing took longer than he expected, but finally Dude lost speed and slowed to a head-shaking halt. Neil had proven to himself that the system did work, sort of, and that he did have some level of control.

He took Dude on in a running walk until they reached the big rock that marked the end of the first part of the trail. On the path ahead he saw hoof-prints from Cheryl's longer ride the day before with Margot, Honey's owner. If that little old lady could take it further, he thought, why couldn't he? He pressed his legs into Dude's sides.

A short way along the path, Neil saw a thin, wavering column of smoke rising from way up the slope on his right. He pulled Dude up. What could that be from? Poachers wouldn't likely give themselves away by building a fire, but somebody had to be up there. Perhaps it was a cabin. He felt a jab of excitement. Maybe it was Luc's. He'd love to see that! He saw a narrow track leading uphill in the direction of the smoke and turned Dude's head.

The path through the trees was rocky and steep and winding, but well trodden. It was probably a deer path, maybe a people path too. It shouldn't be too much of a challenge, he thought, for a strong, surefooted horse like Dude. He leaned forward to take the weight off Dude's back and drove him uphill, at the trot where possible, until they rounded a bend and were suddenly stopped by a fallen pine blocking the path.

Neil hadn't done any real jumping yet, but he had gone over the low training bars, and Ken had shown him how to sit and handle the reins.

He took Dude a little way back down the hill, pointed him at the tree trunk, and drove him on at the trot, pressing in his heels and making a clicking noise at just the right moment. It worked! Dude took the jump, and Neil managed not to fall off.

He was a natural! It was brilliant to be able to do all this after so few lessons. He grinned to himself and took up his quest again. The smell of smoke, and the sight of it rising above the trees just ahead, told him he was nearly there.

He pulled up at the edge of a clearing. He had been right. There was indeed a log cabin, and it had to be Luc's. With Dude's sides heaving under him,

Neil sat back in the saddle and studied the little building. How pretty it looked amongst the trees, he thought, with its red, corrugated-iron roof, silvery horizontal logs, and an amber glow already showing in the small front window. If only he'd brought his paints! He wished he could knock on the door and be asked in for a visit, but he knew that Luc was too panicky for that. He took a last look around, and froze.

A lime-green mountain bike was propped against the side of the cabin.

He stared in disbelief and then heard a familiar yap from inside the cabin. Keeper! Cheryl couldn't know about this. She and Ken were both very strict about Neil not riding alone, and they would be furious. He'd probably be banned from ever riding again. Desperately hoping no one would look out the window and see him, Neil turned Dude around and scuttled away.

Dude picked his way down, breathing more easily now, and they were soon comfortably far from the cabin. Getting down the steeper stretches of the narrow, twisting path, however, was a lot more difficult than going up.

He remembered Cheryl's lesson on how to ride a horse down a sharp slope, and gripped

Dude's barrel tightly with his legs, leaning back to provide ballast. At the same time he saw that Cheryl was right, that the horse would be the best judge of how to handle the drops and turns and rocky outcrops. All he had to do was to keep his own grip and balance and provide firm, reassuring contact with the bit. At the fallen tree, he urged Dude on and managed to keep his seat by grabbing the mane.

The slope flattened out a little, so Neil sat straighter and went faster until a low-hanging branch brushed his eye and he teared up. He blinked away his tears and looked at his watch. There would be plenty of time before dark—and before Ken got back. He relaxed in the saddle and took his feet out of the stirrups to stretch his legs and wriggle his freezing toes.

Crack! The sound of a gunshot ricocheted off the surrounding rocks.

Dude jumped and skittered and took off downhill.

Neil struggled to keep his seat and hold Dude back, desperately angling his feet to regain the lost stirrups. He had just managed to catch the second stirrup with the tip of his boot, and had almost halted Dude, when a stag, wild-eyed and heavy-antlered, crashed out of the trees and leaped across the path, right in front of Dude's nose.

Dude reared so fast and so high, he would have fallen over backwards if Neil hadn't let go of the reins.

Neil fell back and felt his foot twist under him as he landed, his head thumping the ground.

chapter 17

NEIL OPENED HIS EYES ON A CIRCLE of dense, dark firs crowding around him under a gray sky. He tried to sit up and felt a fierce pain in his ankle. He looked behind and saw the path, and the fallen tree far up the hill, and remembered it all: the cabin, the lime-green bike, the downhill getaway, and the gunshot.

He looked at his feet, surprised to see the stirrup, plus its leather strap, still attached to one boot. He squeezed his eyes shut and swallowed, still woozy from shock, then leaned forward to loosen the agonizingly tight laces of his other boot. Had he sprained his ankle, he wondered, or even broken it, when he landed on these rocks? How would he get back?

He thought about what a long and painful trek it would be to get down to the trail, and how far it was after that to the stable. He checked his watch. Ten to four. It would be dark long before he got back. He shivered. Where was Dude? If anything happened to that horse, Ken would never forgive him.

Miserably, he imagined what could have gone wrong. Dude could have fallen and broken a leg during his panicky downhill rush through the trees, or he could have got broken-winded from all that running. There were a million ways he could have been injured.

At least the gate and the stable door had been left open, he remembered, so Dude would be able to find the safety of his stall—if he got that far. Neil steeled himself. He had to get down somehow and see that Dude was all right.

He managed to pull himself up against a tree-trunk and cautiously put his injured foot to the ground. He gasped with the pain. There was no way that foot could bear any weight. And realistically, he saw, there was no way he could hop back to Ken's. Nor would he be able to walk back up to Luc's cabin, embarrassing as that would be.

He sank down again and leaned his back against the tree, pain radiating from his ankle, as he considered his situation. He was in deep trouble. In danger, even. It would be getting dark soon and felt like rain, or even snow. He was shuddering with shock and cold, and the temperature was dropping. Worse still, wolves prowled the forest. He knew; he'd heard them at night. There were bears out here too, people said. Scalding tears spilled down his cheeks and his diaphragm jerked with suppressed sobs as he heard his own voice cry out into the silence, high and scared like that of a little kid: "Mom!"

He dashed his tears away and tried to get a grip on himself. He was not a little kid, and he was not going to just lie there and die. The cabin was not all that far away, he thought, and Cheryl and Luc might hear him if he yelled loud enough.

"Help!" He threw back his head and shouted until his throat felt shredded, his only reply the indignant nattering of a red squirrel, the whooshing of the wind in the treetops, and the jeering of far-off crows.

He looked at his watch again and up at the sky. Nearly four o'clock and the light was beginning to fade. There was nothing for it. He was going to have to crawl back to the cabin.

He got onto his hands and knees and set off. He tried keeping his ankle off the ground while struggling uphill, but it was so difficult and painful he had to keep stopping. His foot throbbed unbearably and kept catching on stones and roots. He felt like throwing up and, in spite of his efforts, was still terribly cold.

After about half an hour of agony, he stopped, shivering and dead beat. If he could just close his eyes and rest for a little while, he decided, he might be more up to the struggle. That red-brown patch of trampled dried ferns beside the path, probably a deer bed judging by the droppings around it, looked comfortable. A dusty whiff of summer rose from the rustling ferns as he curled up in them and gave himself up to sleep.

He was home, safe and warm in his comfortable bed in Vancouver with its soft sheets and cozy duvet, but it seemed that somebody kept calling him.

"Time to wake up, Neil!" the gentle, encouraging voice was saying from somewhere in the

distance. "Do not go back to sleep. Wake up, Neil!
Wake up!"

He groaned, trying to escape back into the safe warm happy feeling, but the voice gave him no break until he opened his eyes and slowly and painfully sat up, shuddering with cold.

He looked in surprise at the stony path beside him, wet and icy in the freezing rain now falling, and then he looked up and down the steep hill. He remembered everything that had happened and put his head in his hands with a groan.

What had he done? He felt guilty and ashamed of himself for taking Dude and going off on his own like that. This was bad, and he'd surely have to pay for it in some way. But something else was eating at him, he knew, something much worse and much deeper, something that was not going to let him go.

He sat in the freezing rain amongst the rocks in the beaten-down bracken under the trees, numb with cold and in serious pain, and faced up to the truth. When he'd cried for his mother back there, down the hill, he hadn't been calling for Jessica. He'd been calling for Sasha, and it was Sasha's voice that had woken him from his near-frozen sleep.

A memory came of her reading him a story, years ago, about an explorer who had lain down, exhausted, to sleep in the snow. He'd been shaken awake by an Inuit hunter who'd made him get up. "If you let yourself go to sleep when you are freezing cold," the hunter said, "you will die. If you want to survive, you have to keep moving."

He thought once again, with shame, about how he had called Sasha names to win Ken's favour.

He knew he didn't think Sasha was a freak. She was his mother, no question about it. She had lied to him, sure, but how could he blame her? Her own father had turned her away, and still said terrible things about her. Why wouldn't she be afraid to tell her only son the truth?

The worst thing of all was that Neil had proven her right. He had treated her terribly. He'd caused her accident and then run away and tried to forget her. He'd ignored the love she'd given him all these years. She had always put him first, and he had taken that completely for granted.

He knew now that he still loved and needed her. She was his mother, and she was all he had. She had deceived him, certainly, but she hadn't done it to be mean. She had probably put it off, time and again, unsure of how to explain it to him, afraid of his reaction.

For the first time, Neil thought about what Sasha's life must have been like. Years of fear and shame and secrets. He wondered if she had always known that she was a woman. He wished that she was here, so he could ask her.

He turned to look at the trail he'd just made. He seemed to have come quite a long way, considering. He must be at least halfway to the cabin. He couldn't give up now. Shaking with cold, he got back on his hands and knees. He gritted his teeth against the pain and set off once more.

Ten agonizing minutes later, he took stock again: Dragging himself uphill over the icy roots and stones was getting impossible. His jeans had long ago given way at his already bleeding knees, and his hands in their beat-up gloves were raw and freezing. He could feel himself getting weaker and disoriented. He even believed at one point that the fallen tree-trunk was still ahead of him, when he had already got himself over it.

He longed to just lie down and sleep, even more than last time, but he remembered Sasha's story and forced himself to keep going, a little bit at a time, and managed to cover several metres more.

He must be close to the cabin now, he thought. He should try another shout. He raised himself up on his knees, threw back his head, and put all his remaining strength into his cry: "Help! Cheryl! Luc! Help me!"

chapter 18

NEIL WAS IN A BIG SOFT ARMCHAIR beside an old wood stove, its doors open to show a glowing fire. He was propped up by pillows, a patchwork quilt tucked around him. His foot and ankle, freed of the boot and wrapped in an ice-cold towel, rested on a cushioned stool.

"We were already out looking for you," Cheryl said. She knelt beside his chair with Luc standing behind her. "We were looking for someone, anyways, because we didn't know it was you then, did we?" She looked up at Luc, who shook his head. "We'd heard the gunshot but didn't think nothing of it, because it happens a lot these days. But Keeper here," she pointed to the little dog toasting himself in front of the stove, "he kept listening and whining, and clawing at the door like he heard something, so in the end we let him out, and he took off like a bullet and then came running back barking and looking back downhill. So we knew something was up. Right, Luc?"

Luc nodded and leaned down to stroke Keeper's ears.

"Then we seen the hoofprints going down the hill," Cheryl said, "and Keeper was still racing up and down barking, so we set off after him, and then my cellphone rang and it was Ken, saying he'd just got home to find Dude in the stable all tacked up and still in a lather. He reckoned you must have taken him out and had a fall but he couldn't find you nowheres, so I was to come and help him look. So then I reckoned the hoofprints had to be Dude's."

She took a big breath and stood up. "By then Keeper was barking like crazy further down the hill, so we ran to see, and there you were!"

She glared at him, fists on hips. "You were lucky, Neil. You should just be happy this didn't happen in winter! What were you thinking of anyways, going off on Dude by yourself?"

Luc shook his head at Cheryl, a finger to his lips, before leading her away to sit at the table.

Neil looked dopily around. The room was like a dream, a real old-style cabin, its wide logs chinked with plaster, a rough plank floor, small high windows with red gingham curtains, and a door that looked solid enough to resist a bear. His mom would love this, he thought, the way the oil lamp threw a warm golden light on the rough pine table, two wooden chairs, and a small hutch.

The Classic Car calendar on the wall beside the window was the one from the convenience store, same as the one Ken had in the barn. Wooden shelves ran along the walls, the ones beside the loaded hutch crowded with cans and cartons and jars of food. A saucepan and a blackened frying pan sat on the shelf beside the stove, with ladles hanging from hooks underneath. The shelf over the bed was piled up with books and magazines, along with a transistor radio. Neil painfully turned his head and saw a wooden four-poster bed filling about a quarter of the room.

A mouth-watering smell came from a pot on the stove, mixed with that of wet wool from his clothes drying on a rack nearby, and of wet dog from Keeper.

His ankle hurt brutally and he was aching all over, especially his shoulder and head, but he was not going to die. He would have to face Ken, but he was alive and warm and safe—and so, he gathered, thanking his lucky stars, was Dude. Better still, in spite of the pain, Neil actually felt strangely happy, as if a tight painful knot had been loosened in his chest.

Cheryl made him follow her finger with his eyes for some reason, and answer questions, like what was his name, and where did he live, and so on. "Here," she said when she was finished, "take this Tylenol. It'll help with the pain." From the tall enamel jug by the door, she poured water into a cup which she handed to him with the tablet.

"Here's the thing, see, Neil," she said. "Nick from the store's gonna come up here in his Jeep to get you down to the main road, where Ken will be waiting with the truck to take you to the hospital."

He swallowed the pill. "But how can Nick get up here?"

Cheryl and Luc exchanged a grin. "No problem, kiddo!" she said. "We're real close to the old logging road. It's just a bit further up and over that way. If you'd stayed on the trail, you'd have hit it in no time. Anyways, in a while, me and Luc's gonna get you up to the old road to meet Nick."

She took a small enamel saucepan off the stove to pour something creamy into a thick blue mug. "Here. Drink this chicken noodle soup. It'll make you feel a whole lot better. And then I'll phone the guys and we'll get you dressed, ready to go."

The soup was the most delicious thing Neil had ever tasted. He felt stronger with every mouthful. If it hadn't been for that stupid hunter, he thought as he slurped it down, or if he'd only known about the logging road, he could have gotten away with the whole thing. Nothing ever worked out the way he thought it would. He gulped down the salty, slippery noodles before resigning himself to the agony of getting dressed and being carried off to meet Ken.

At the junction, Luc, who was surprisingly strong, practically lifted Neil into the Jeep. He gently settled him into the passenger's seat and looked into his eyes before closing the door. *"Bon chance,"* he said. "Good luck."

***

"Thank God it's only six o'clock," Ken said grimly as they sat in the rapidly filling Emergency waiting room. "It's bad enough as it is, but it always gets real busy on Saturday night."

Neil slumped on a hard chair, still in serious pain and surrounded by coughs and groans and muttered curses. He stared miserably at the dirty floor. Ken was really mad at him. He'd hardly said a word all the way to the hospital and had not been gentle in getting him out of the truck and into the waiting room.

"Sorry, Ken," he muttered. "I shouldn't have taken Dude out."

"You're darn right you shouldn't have," Ken almost shouted.

The skinny woman next to them looked up in fright from her sleeping baby.

"You could've ruined my best horse!" Ken said. "He was all lathered up and still pretty spooked when I found him in the barn. I'll probably have to get the vet to check his lungs."

He turned his back on Neil, saying over his shoulder, "Fine thanks I get, eh?"

Neil slumped further. The baby set up an ear-splitting wail, yanked the soother out of its mouth, and flung it into the middle of the room. An old man coughed, non-stop, while a hairy guy in the far corner talked loudly to himself, swearing and gesticulating.

Neil heard his name called and stood up to hobble gratefully away on the crutches brought by the nurse.

The X-ray technician was so kind and gentle she made him want to cry. "Doesn't look too bad," she said. "It's very good that the swelling was kept down." She helped him into a wheelchair to be taken to the doctor.

After an awkwardly silent few minutes with Ken, the doctor arrived to study the X-ray.

"It's a good clean break," he said, "More of a fracture really, since nothing's out of place. See?" The doctor pointed to the thin line across the bottom of the bigger leg bone in the transparency up on the wall. "We'll soon get you fixed up." He looked at Neil. "How did this happen, anyway?"

"Fell off a horse," Neil mumbled under Ken's icy stare.

The orderly wheeled him down a long corri-
dor to a room where a small, amazingly freckled
man with the reddest hair Neil had ever seen set
about putting his throbbing ankle in a cast, first
putting it in a sort of sock, and then wrapping it in
heavy bandages soaked in ice-cold Plaster of Paris.

"It should dry in about twenty minutes," the
man said. "Be very careful for the first couple of
days and whatever you do, don't get it wet. No
showers, right?"

An hour later, painkillers in his pocket, Neil
sat miserably beside Ken as the truck bumped its
way back to the stable.

"Can't very well stay here with a broken
ankle, can you?" Ken said finally. "And anyway,
she wants you back right away. Sasha, that is. She's
flying here to get you as soon as she gets the doc's
clearance. Should only be a few days." He looked
sternly ahead. "I think it's for the best."

chapter 19

THREE DAYS LATER, AS NEIL STOOD by the front window waiting for his mom to arrive, he saw his grandfather hobble up to his truck, keys in hand. Was he going somewhere? With Sasha arriving any minute? The guy was unbelievable.

Neil threw open the front door, managed the steps with difficulty, and swung along on his crutches to confront Ken. "Where are you going? Aren't you even going to say hello to my mom?" he asked furiously. *And goodbye to me*, he felt like adding.

"I've got important business in town," Ken said, jangling the keys. "And I'm gonna be late. Sorry. Gotta rush."

"But my mom's going to be here any minute, Ken. She phoned to say she's on her way from the airport. Couldn't you call and say you'll be a bit late? I mean this is *important*." He could feel the sweat forming on his forehead and upper lip.

"Not my scene," said Ken, opening the truck door. He gave Neil a quick pat on the arm. "Goodbye, buddy. Take care." Then he got in, slammed the door, and was gone, rattling off down the drive. Neil glared after him as the truck turned onto the road and drove off.

A few moments later, he saw his mom finally drive up slowly in a small rental car and pull in behind the clump of cedars by the gate. She stayed there, half hidden, for at least ten minutes. She must be bracing herself to meet her rotten father again, he thought, and also to have to face an angry son. She wouldn't be meeting Ken, and she wouldn't have to meet an angry son either, but she didn't know that yet.

There was still no sign of movement from the car.

Neil felt so mad at Ken that if it hadn't been for the crutches, he would have kicked or punched something. His mom was a good person. She didn't deserve to be treated like that, like she didn't matter.

Finally, the car moved. His mom looked so thin and pale and anxious as she closed the gate, he wished he was in good enough shape to at least do that for her. It was awfully soon after her accident. When the car pulled up in front of the bungalow, he flung open the front door and hopped through on his crutches, preparing to attempt the steps.

"Wait, Neil! I'm coming!" She jumped out of the car and hurried up the steps, holding out her arms to stop him before he could begin the risky manoeuvre. He saw how her hair was growing back in what looked like a soft, dense crewcut.

"Hi, Mom." Neil stood awkwardly on his crutches while she hugged him. He could feel how soft and smooth the skin of her cheek was, and could smell her familiar perfume.

She stood back to look him over and pulled a sympathetic face at the sight of the cast. "Oh, Neil! Poor you!" she said, and then laughed. "But how could you have grown so much in less than two weeks? You look different already!"

He grinned and hopped around to point a crutch at Cheryl, lurking behind him in the doorway. "Mom, this is Cheryl. Cheryl, this is my mom, Sasha."

"Pleased to meet you." He saw Cheryl's eyes slide over his mom's face to settle on some distant point. "Come in and make yourself at home," she said, waving a hand towards the sofa under the window. "I'll go make us some coffee."

"Are you okay to drive so soon, Mom?" Neil asked as they sat waiting for Cheryl to return. "Couldn't Margaret have come with you?"

"I wanted to have this quiet time alone with you," she said. "It's a quick drive from the airport to here, and the doctor said it should be okay if I take it easy. My headaches are gone and I've been driving around for a few days now. The main thing is to get you back on your two feet, right?" She gave him a small smile.

"I like your hair," Neil said, examining the startling white flash. "That white bit is cool!"

She cautiously touched the patch at the V of her hairline.

"Sorry!" He felt himself blush. "That's from the accident, isn't it, from when you hurt your head." He bent to scratch his shin just above the plaster cast. "What was it like, the accident? Do you remember how it happened?" He looked up. "Can you tell me about it?"

She smoothed her skirt." I didn't remember anything for a few days, Neil, but then it all came back to me." She thought for a bit. "I remember it was dark and very windy," she said, "and raining hard. The streets were shining wet under the streetlights, and I could see people bent over, struggling with their umbrellas in the wind." She shook her head and took a big breath.

"Anyway, I raced down Laurier, hoping to make the left turn onto Elgin before the lights changed, and to shake off the tailgater who was half-blinding me, and I'd just got around on the orange, when an umbrella slammed into my windshield!" She squeezed her eyes tight shut at the memory. "Of course I couldn't see a thing, and I thought I'd hit someone, so I stood on the brakes."

Opening her eyes wide, she went on, "And that's all I remember. I gather the tailgater smashed into me at about the same time as another car crashed into me from the side." She pulled a face. "I didn't have my seat belt on, so my head hit something." She felt at the scar on her head. "My knees were pretty banged up too, but no bones were broken, except for the crack in my skull."

"You didn't have your seat belt on, Mom? You used to freak out if I didn't do mine up, even if we were still in the garage."

"No. Well, I didn't even think about it. I was so desperate to find you I just drove—the way we all used to when I was young."

She looked hard at him. "You know, I ran after you, Neil, when you dashed off, but you were already out of sight...so I drove to your school, thinking you might have caught the bus and gone back there. Anyway, a boy there told me to try the Rideau Mall, so I drove there and went to the food court, knowing you'd be hungry. A man there with a little boy thought he'd seen you. He said you left with a girl." She leaned back and closed her eyes.

"So anyway," she sat up and went on, "I drove around some more, to look for you, and then I went home in case you were there, but of course you weren't." She shook her head. "I kind of lost it after that and drove frantically around, and that's when I had the crash."

"So I guess you only just missed us, Mom."
He frowned. "It's weird, isn't it, to think what a
difference those couple of minutes made? None
of this would have happened if Courtenay and
me had still been at the food court when you
got there." He rubbed a shiny patch on the
arm of the couch. "I wouldn't have caused your
accident."

She sat up quickly. "No, Neil! None of this
was your fault. I was the one to blame." She wrung
her hands. "I did everything wrong. I was planning to tell you the whole story that night, but it
all went horribly wrong." She gave him a quick,
almost shy look. "I just wish you knew how much
you mean to me, Neil, despite all that."

He looked away. "I think I do, Mom," he
said, "and I even think I understand why you felt
you couldn't tell me the truth from the start, but
still..." his voice trailed off as he looked back at
her.

Neil's mother stared at him as if she wasn't
sure she recognized him, and opened her mouth
to say something when a thump at the door made
her look around, her hand flying to her chest.

Neil stumped over to open the door for
Keeper and saw his mother slump back, deflated.

He felt more disgusted than ever at Ken as he watched her try to cover her disappointment by petting the dog.

"What a cutie! Is this the dog that rescued you?" She looked up from Keeper, who was twirling with excitement.

"Yup. This is Keeper. He's the biggest little dog you're ever going to see." Neil watched happily as she played with the dog while they waited for the coffee.

Cheryl kept her eyes on the loaded tray as she carried it over and set it down on the wooden toolbox that did for a coffee table. "Ken says to tell you he's sorry he couldn't be here to meet you," she said, fussing with the mugs, "but he has an appointment in town this morning."

After a pause, Sasha shrugged and managed a small, twisted smile. She watched Cheryl fill three large mugs with coffee. "So, you drink coffee now, Neil?" she said. "I guess you're not a little kid anymore." As his mom took the mug, Neil saw Cheryl's eyes fix on her long, dark-red nails before shifting to her face and then flicking away to the window.

"We're sure gonna miss young Neil," Cheryl said, her eyes now on the dented metal coffee pot.

"He's a fast learner and a real good worker. You should see this guy on a horse! I've never known anyone who picked it up so quick!" She frowned and put her mug down. "Of course he brought all this on himself," she gestured at the crutches, "so it's a good thing he's going home." She looked at Neil briefly before returning to her coffee. "We were starting to forget that he's still just a kid."

chapter 20

"COME AND SEE THE HORSES, Mom." Neil said as they finished their coffee. "They're just outside in the paddock."

"How many horses do you have here?" his mom asked as they stood looking out at the door.

"Three horses, two big ponies, and a Shetland," said Cheryl, coming up alongside them.

"And the donkey," Neil said, "Benjamin."

"You and that donkey!" Looking into the distance, Cheryl said, "Ken might be getting rid of the whole lot actually."

Neil stared at her. "He's going to sell them?" He felt his mouth twisting. "All of them?"

"Yup. Guess he has to," Cheryl said. "Not enough money coming in." She turned in Sasha's direction to explain, still without looking at her: "The lady that owns that little quarter horse there, she's finally gonna give up riding. And the girls those two paint ponies belong to need the money for university now. None of the little kids want to ride the Shetland no more, not since he wiped one of them off on a fence post. And now the owner of that big black one's giving up on him too."

"But what about Dude?" Neil asked, blinking furiously.

Cheryl smiled at him. "Don't you worry about Dude, kid. Ken's already found a good home for him, and you'll be happy to hear that your precious Benjamin's going with him. There's a real nice girl that's had her eye on Dude for the last year or so. Good little rider too. You know who I mean, Neil. Amelie. You were watching them jump in the ring last week.

He did know the girl. Small and slim, and a very competent rider; she'd looked good on Dude. It had even occurred to Neil as he watched that he might be getting a bit too tall for the horse. But of course he'd had no idea then what Ken had in mind.

Cheryl shrugged. "Nope, it looks like the end of the road for the stable, unless somebody buys the whole shebang," she said. "Ken's getting on a bit now anyways, and his arthritis sure ain't getting any better. And me, I'm out of here just as soon as I can find work somewheres else."

"You're leaving?" Without either of them, how would Ken manage?

"Yup, I'm off. Me and Ken had a bit of a falling out Sunday night, after your accident." She picked Keeper up for a rough cuddle.

Neil thought he'd heard raised voices in the kitchen that night. He had a pretty good idea what the fight was about.

"Tell my mom how Keeper saved me, Cheryl," he said, looking hard at her and then glancing over at his mom and back, trying to convey that Cheryl should look at his mom when speaking to her.

As Cheryl proudly explained how brilliant Keeper had been, he saw how she began glancing over the dog's head at his mom for approval.

But Neil had to know more about Ken selling up. He stretched his chin and swallowed. "What about Mackie?" he asked.

She grinned. "That little devil's so darn cute, he'll find an owner. Maybe he'd be better off anyways with just one rider."

"And what about the cat?"

"Oh, she'll survive. There's plenty of mice in the barn."

"But she's pregnant. She needs looking after." He looked at his mom. "Doesn't she?"

Cheryl laughed, putting Keeper back down. "She's had kittens before. She'll manage just fine. She's got a barn to live in, and plenty of fresh food running around for free. Ken knows she's there, and I'll check in on her from time to time."

"Maybe," Sasha said, looking up from Keeper, "if there's a carrier here we could have, we could take the cat back home with us, if you'd like, Neil. It's not such a long flight."

He looked at her in amazement.

"Are you nuts?" said Cheryl. "Have you ever travelled with a cat? She'd yowl non-stop the whole darn way. And poop like you wouldn't believe. I had to take her to the vet once, and I promise you, I'll not be doing that again."

"No, Mom," Neil said, smiling, "Cheryl's right. This cat isn't tame and trusting like Perkins. He knows all about going in the car, but she's half wild and she'd be terrified, and anyway it's too long a trip. She's definitely better off staying here."

His mom sat back, looking relieved.

Cheryl got up. "Well, I better get back to work. Morning chores and all that." Looking straight at Neil's mom, she shook her hand warmly. "Take your time here, Sasha. No rush. It was real nice meeting you. Have a safe trip back." Turning to Neil, she said, "Don't forget us now."

"No way." He stood up. "And...well, thanks for everything, Cheryl."

Balanced on one leg Neil gave her a clumsy hug, smelling the stable on her clothes and cigarette smoke in her hair. "Say goodbye and thank you to Luc for me," he said, his good leg suddenly feeling shaky.

chapter 21

*T*HE LINDA ROCK LOOMED UP IN front of Neil and Sasha as they drove towards Saint John on their way to the airport. Neil saw his mom turn her head as they went by and remembered how he'd felt when he first saw those words. Had she ever felt like that about anyone, he wondered, that she would love them forever?

"What do you think about that?" he said from the back seat as they turned towards the highway. "Those words back there on the rock?"

In the rear-view mirror he saw her raise her eyebrows and blink while keeping her eyes on the road. "I think it's beautiful," she said over the thrum of the engine. *Linda I will love you forever.* It's like a poem, with all those l's and v's and i's and o's."

"No, I mean about the meaning. Seriously, can a person ever be as sure as that?"

"Oh yes," she said, "of course they can." She met his eyes in the mirror. "I know that's how I felt about you the first time I saw you."

He stiffened. He hadn't expected she'd want to get into that stuff so soon.

While they waited to merge, she turned around to look at him. "Do you want to talk about that?"

He relaxed enough to shrug and look away. "In a bit, maybe," he said.

They drove in silence until they were clear of Saint John. She looked around again. "Are you ready to talk?"

He pressed himself into the corner of the rear seat, zipped up his hoodie, and crossed his arms. He did want to know, of course. Everything. But not right now. Maybe she could put it in a letter or something, so that he could take it all in at his own pace when he was by himself. But he could tell from the set of her mouth and her nervous glances in the mirror that wasn't going to happen. This was it. He closed his eyes. "If you want."

"Jessica and I were in love," she said, "but I had to leave her because I was pretending to be someone I wasn't."

"Oh. I see," he said. He didn't really, but he wanted to.

"I knew I had to change myself," she went on, "not into someone totally different who no longer loved Jessica, but into the hidden person I'd been all along."

"But what about when you were, like, my age?" he asked. "Were you a hidden person then?"

"I was confused by my feelings, but I mostly went along with what people expected of me. I was very good at pretending to be a boy, since I was tall and athletic and girls liked me."

"Wasn't there anyone you could talk to," Neil asked, "like your parents?"

"Huh. Margaret was never unkind, but I couldn't talk to her about those feelings, and I always felt that Ken was like my enemy, always onto me, watching me for any sign of girlishness."

She looked up at a hawk slowly circling over the field. "When I was little, he forced me to have a crewcut and threw away my teddy bear because he said I held it like a girl."

"Oh, that's awful, Mom. You didn't have anyone at all?"

"No, not really. I couldn't even really explain it to myself until I got old enough."

"But you've got me now," Neil said. "And Margaret."

Sasha gave him a sad smile in the mirror.

He thought for a bit. "I'm sorry I was so rough on you, Mom," he said. "I just didn't understand why you wouldn't tell me about my father, and I was getting madder and madder at you. I think I understand better now though." He sat forward. "But what I don't understand is why people are so mean about it all. I mean, if that's the way you are, what's the matter with that?"

She pulled over onto the soft shoulder and stopped the car. "I can't believe I'm talking to you like this, Neil," she turned to look at him, "so openly, and so much on the same wavelength. You're like a different person." She shuffled around to face him more squarely. "I'll go back to all that later if you want, but let's talk about you for a bit."

She held out her hand towards him. "Tell me what happened at Ken's to cause such a change in your attitude toward me."

This was easier. He shifted his cast and put a cushion behind his head before he described the accident on Dude and the frozen dream from which she'd made him wake up.

"That was when I realized," he said, "that you were the only person in my whole life who cared at all about me, except for Margaret, I guess, and maybe..." he stopped and looked away. He wasn't bringing Courtenay into this. Besides, she had just been a friend really.

"Except for...? Except for whom, Neil?" She paused. "Except for *Ken*?"

"*Ken?*" he laughed. "No way! Ken doesn't give a hoot about me, or anyone really. Why would you ever think that?"

She shrugged, smiling. "Well...I guess I was afraid you'd see him as the father figure you've been searching for. And that he would see you as the son he never really had. To be honest, I was jealous and scared stiff, not only of losing you, but of losing you to *him*."

"Well, you didn't need to worry, Mom. Ken couldn't be a father figure if he tried."

Neil frowned. "Honestly though, Mom, he should have stayed at the stable until you came. He should have been there for you."

Sasha looked away across the fields. "He was never there for me," she said. She narrowed her eyes. "Did he ever say anything to you about me?"

Neil decided not to go into that. "Not really. He just seemed uncomfortable with it all." He sat up. "What's the matter with him anyway? Why is he such a total jerk?"

"I don't know, Neil. As far as I can remember, he's always been like that. Margaret says he's lost touch with his own feelings, perhaps because he's afraid of them." She looked at him. "In the end, it's his choice. You can't change people, they can only do that themselves."

He raised his eyebrows and returned her look. He needed to get this straight.

"Mom, why did you lie to me?" he said.

After a long pause, she spoke, looking down at her lap: "I know it was hard for you, Neil. I was very wrong not to tell you the truth sooner. I'm sorry for the way I handled it. I kept telling myself that I should wait until you were older and could understand it all better." She looked up at him. "And what would have been the right age, anyway, for you to learn about that? I didn't know where to begin, and I was so alone in all this, and so horribly afraid of losing you, I just couldn't do it." She sighed. "I know all this must be terribly difficult for you, Neil, but please try to understand."

He nodded seriously. "I am trying, Mom."

***

They arrived at the small, neat airport just in time to return the car and have a lobster roll at the bistro before boarding the plane.

"It's not so bad," his mom said, after they'd buckled themselves into their cramped seats. "We'll be home in time for dinner. Margaret will meet us at the airport."

Neil's stomach contracted. "Is Margaret still mad at me?"

Sasha smiled. "She's over it. She wasn't worried about the mess you left, she was worried about you. There was no real harm done. Just to our nerves!" She opened her purse and took out a bottle of painkillers. She swallowed one, then leaned her head back and closed her eyes. "I'm going to have a bit of a rest now."

Coming here must have been very hard on her, Neil thought, trying to move his injured foot under the seat in front, especially so soon after her accident. No wonder she looked so pale. A sleep would do her good. He felt a bit sleepy himself and tried to get comfortable, putting his foot on Sasha's carry-on bag under the seat ahead, and his head on one of the little pillows Sasha had asked for. The faint vibration and drone of the plane were soothing, and Neil felt calm inside as he closed his tired eyes.

"Cabin crew, prepare for landing," came a sudden loud announcement over the speaker.

As the flight attendant came down the aisle, checking seat belts and reminding people to lift their trays, Neil looked out the window at Ottawa. His new city was getting closer by the moment, and he realized, with some surprise, that he was looking forward to getting back to his life here.

He braced for landing, ready to step back into his new home.

chapter 22

FEET UP ON THE SQUISHY RED couch, Neil was deep into *Great Expectations,* at the part about the cobwebby wedding cake with the blotchy spiders running in and out of it, when his cellphone rang.

"Hi, Neil." The voice sounded familiar. "This is Hiu. Remember me? We used to sit together in French. They told me at school that you'd broken your ankle but you'd be back soon."

"Oh, hey Hiu," said Neil. "How's it going?"

"Pretty good. I just wanted to say hi, and to ask if you feel like getting together at the mall after school."

"Today?" Neil sat up. He would love to meet Hiu again. It seemed years since he'd talked to anyone his own age.

"Sure. We could meet at the food court at, say, four o'clock, and hang out for a bit. Are you up for that?"

"That sounds great."

"Cool. Maybe Courtenay could come too. I know she'd like to see you, since you practically lived next door to each other for a bit, didn't you? Are you okay with that?"

"Uh...sure."

"Okay great, I'll ask her. See you soon."

He would have preferred to take his own time about meeting Courtenay, but the sooner the better. If she didn't turn up, he'd get the message. He settled back down to his book and had just got to the bit where the beautiful Estella turns up her nose at Pip for being a rough, common boy, when the doorbell rang. Compared to the stable, life was a social frenzy here, he thought as he got up to answer it.

"Hello, Neil. It's good to see you again." The small pretty woman standing on the doorstep smiled at him. "I'm Julie. Do you remember me? We met in the hospital."

Sure," he said. It was his mom's nice nurse. Was she here for a home check-up? He opened the door wider. "Would you like to come in?"

"No, I won't, thanks. I'm in a bit of a rush. I just wanted to leave a message for Sasha since her phone is turned off. Would you tell her that I'm sorry, but there's been a change of shifts so I won't be able to swing by this afternoon?"

"Yeah," he said, "I'll tell her."

"Thanks Neil, I'll see you again soon, I'm sure."

He stood in the doorway and watched as she climbed into a light blue car and took off.

So, his mom had invited Julie to visit them that afternoon? Could this mean something? He wasn't sure how he felt about that.

Apart from the pain in his ankle, Neil had to admit he was very comfortable here in this bright colourful house, with his mom once again "waiting on him hand and foot," as Ken and Cheryl would put it. It was quite a change from his life at the stable.

Neil missed the animals, of course, especially Dude and Keeper, but he knew very well that he was finally in a good place. He was glad to be back, glad to be returning to school soon, especially now that Hiu had called him. Most of all, he was happy to be in a much better relationship with his mom.

"All I want to do now," she had said, "is to look after you and try to make it up to you." At the time, he'd thought this sounded great, but maybe this thing with Julie was good. Could be it was time his mom had a life of her own.

***

"Hey, man! Welcome back!" Hiu clapped Neil on the back, grinning. "How are you doing? You were pretty easy to spot." He pointed at Neil's crutches. "Let's go over there for you to be safer." They moved around a corner to be out of the crush of kids. "How long do you have to be on those?"

"Not sure," Neil said. "Tomorrow I get to see the doctor about ordering a special boot that's supposed to make getting around a lot easier. I'll be back at school on Monday."

"That's great. How long will your ankle take to heal?"

"The doctor in Saint John said it should mend perfectly and quickly if I'm careful and don't rush it. But it's going to take another six weeks at least, and then I'll still have to go slow."

"Sounds good, though. Do you think you'll be up for track and field by the summer? We were both going to try out, remember?"

"Yeah, I hope so. I want to play soccer too, later, next year maybe, when my ankle's better."

"Me too. Come on, let's get in line for a drink. Courtenay will be here any minute."

"Great..." he grinned at Hiu. "Listen. I'll get it. My mom gave me some money. She's going to pick me up at five because she thinks the bus would be difficult with these." He shifted the crutch.

"Hi guys." Courtenay appeared in front of them in her long black coat. "How are you doing, Neil?" She looked just the same, except a bit neater. Her hair was fastened back and looked a lot tidier, and the dangling button on her coat had been fixed. She was smiling at him.

"Gimme the money before you get knocked over, Neil," Hiu said, anxiously watching a couple of guys shoving and pushing each other nearby. "Why don't you two go grab a seat while I get the drinks."

"You okay?" Courtenay asked as they slipped into a space left on the bench by an old lady with a lot of bags.

"Look, Courtenay, I'm sorry," he blurted out, anxious to get this over with before Hiu came back. "I was really rude to you, and I know you were just trying to help me. I've been feeling terrible about that."

"Forget about it," she said. "You were upset, and I don't blame you." She looked at him seriously. "How are you now?"

"I'm okay, actually." He said, still surprised to realize it was true.

"Really?" She raised her eyebrows.

"Yeah. Really." They shifted over to make room for Hiu.

"You know I'm...living at Margaret's now?" she said to him before slurping her drink.

"You're what?" No one had said anything about this to him. "How did that happen?"

"Yes, well just after you ran off, my mom and dad had a huge fight, and the police came and took my dad away, and my mom was in a real state, so Margaret came and said for me to come home with her."

"Wow! But what happened then to your mom and dad?"

"Well, after they let him go, my dad went to stay with his mom in Florida, and believe it or not, my mom is getting help. She'll be away for a few months, but it's for the best. And it's all thanks to Margaret. She said I could live with her until my mom gets back."

"Ha!" This was good news. "So you're going to be around quite a bit?"

"Guess so. I'm so lucky! Margaret's so kind to me, and it's nice and peaceful living with her."

As they sat chatting, Neil looked around and remembered his first visit to the mall. What a lot had happened since then, he thought. Maybe he really was becoming a different person.

chapter 23

NEIL AND HIS MOM HURRIED UP TO
Margaret's door. He knew from the loving
way his grandmother had greeted him at the
airport that she had somehow totally forgiven
him for trashing her home. And now, just a few
days later, she was giving a big dinner to celebrate his return. He wasn't sure if he deserved
any of it.

She opened the door, smiling happily. "That
which was lost, is found," she exclaimed, giving

him a big hug. He returned it as well as he could. His mouth was dry and he couldn't think of what to say. "Hi, Grandma," he croaked.

She looked almost pretty that evening, not nearly so old, with her hair short and wavy, and a bit of colour on her lips and cheeks.

He looked around. The living room seemed larger and lighter, he thought, probably because the heavy lace drapes had been replaced by plainer, more transparent ones. Otherwise it was all much the same. Even the painting was back, hanging in its old spot once again.

He took a flat brown-paper parcel from Sasha's carrier bag and offered it to Margaret. "This is for you," he said.

She pulled off the wrappings and held up the framed sketch. "Oh, how extraordinary," she said. "It's a picture of Old Dude. Look, Sasha." She held up the drawing. "This is Old Dude to the life, isn't it?"

Sasha went over to see it better. "It sure is," she said. "It's the image of him." She leaned forward, examining it. "This is a very good drawing, Neil—the best thing I've seen you do so far. The perspective is really well done, and I love how you've caught that soft look in his eye."

She squinted at the drawing. "It's Old Dude all right." She frowned suddenly and looked up. "But how can he possibly be still alive? I mean all that was at least thirty years ago, and he was old then."

"It's Little Dude actually," he explained, feeling very proud. "He's Old Dude's grandson. Ken says he's pretty much a clone. I remembered that you really liked that horse, Grandma, so I put this in a frame I found in the barn."

"Thank you, Neil," Margaret said. "It's wonderful." She propped it up on the desk in the corner.

The doorbell rang, and a moment later someone called from the entry: "Hello! It's me, Julie."

He'd seen Julie at home during these last few days, but each time she'd been in uniform, coming from or going to work. She looked different now, all dressed up in a floaty white and gold dress, but oddly enough, more ordinary, like someone who might live on their street or be some little kid's mother. She went over to hug Sasha, and they shared a quick kiss before she turned to Neil with a big smile.

"How are *you* today?" Julie said. "You know, I think you've grown in the last couple of days." She laughed. "I remember my young brother shooting up like that when he was your age. It's amazing how fast kids grow, especially boys."

"It certainly is," Margaret said. "And change. I can hardly believe it's the same boy. But come and look at this, Julie."

While they looked at the drawing, Neil watched his mom sit down again in the comfy armchair and lean her head back, her eyes closed and a slight smile formed on her lips. She was still pale, but her face looked somehow softer. The worry lines were nearly gone from between her eyebrows and around her mouth; she looked a bit tired, but sort of peaceful and beautiful.

With a clink and a clatter, Margaret and Julie were setting the table, now made into an oval by its big central leaf. He watched them set out side plates, napkins, and silverware, along with the fancy wine glasses from the corner cabinet. He heard the unmistakable clunk of the fridge door and knew that must be Courtenay in the kitchen.

His mouth watered at the good smells coming from there. Margaret had roasted a large chicken for the dinner, plus all the trimmings: stuffing, roast potatoes, mashed sweet potatoes, Brussels sprouts, gravy, and red-currant jelly.

Taking in these aromas and the gleaming table settings, and hearing the laughter and comfortable chatter going on behind him, Neil suddenly thought of Ken, all by himself in his miserable little bungalow. He couldn't help feeling a bit sorry for his grandfather. He was what he was, and maybe couldn't change. In his own way, Ken had helped Neil; he had taught him a lot—about riding and looking after horses anyway, which was something after all. Maybe someday, he'd give Ken a call.

A sound like a gunshot, followed by laughter, came from the kitchen. Margaret hurried back into the room with Julie. "Everything's keeping hot in the oven," she said, "but first, we're going to celebrate the return of the prodigal son with a toast!"

"Prodigal son?" he said. "A toast?"

"Just a spot. Why not? Here comes Courtenay with it now—champagne for the grown-ups and sparkling grape juice for you two!"

Courtenay looked even prettier than Neil remembered, in a black turtleneck and pants. She carried a round silver tray on which five tall thin glasses ringed a fat, gold-wired bottle and a slim, dark green one. She placed it on the side table next to Sasha and sat by Julie on the loveseat, getting a welcoming hug and kiss.

After they had all been provided with their equally sparkling drinks, Margaret tapped a fork against her glass. "Here's to us," she said, looking around with a smile. They raised their glasses. "We've all been through a lot lately," she said, "one way or another, but here we all are, safe and happy and, most important, together. So, here's to love, and kindness, and courage."

Neil looked over at Courtenay and raised his glass higher. The silver ball on her lip flashed as she smiled and tilted her glass towards his.

"Isn't it Neil's fourteenth birthday soon?" Julie asked.

"November the twentieth," Sasha said. She turned to him. "I've been wondering, Neil..." she looked at him uncertainly, "what would you like for your birthday? Since you love horses so much, I was thinking about riding lessons—after your ankle's mended of course. Would you like that?"

That all belonged to a different part of his life, he thought, a part that was over. Besides, riding lessons would seem rather tame after what he'd experienced.

"I don't think so, Mom," he said, "although maybe I'll take it up again some time." He hesitated. "I was wondering though, after I saw how much you liked Keeper...." He stared into the bubbles before looking up. "How would you feel about us getting a dog?"

He saw Julie clasp her hands while Margaret gave a slow, thoughtful smile. Courtenay was looking at Sasha, her eyes wide and her lips pressed together as if holding her breath.

"I'd look after it," he said, "with walks and feeds and that. And it would be company for you, Mom, on days when you're not working and I'm at school. And it could be protection for you, too, when you go running." He took a breath. "We could get a rescue dog. That way you can sort of tell what you're getting, and it would already be house-trained, so it wouldn't be too much trouble for you, and it wouldn't cost all that much either."

"Relax, Neil!" Sasha laughed. "You got me at the mention of Keeper. I think it's a great idea. Get yourself a bit more mobile," she nodded at his cast, "and when you're ready, we'll do it. In the meantime you can do some research online to see what sort of dog you think we should get."

He smiled. Maybe a really big dog, he thought, like a German shepherd or a golden retriever. Or a Great Dane. Or they could get a rescued boxer. Or even a Jack Russell puppy. That was it! He could read all about training and sign up for obedience school.

Margaret stood. "To the table, everyone!"

As they moved to take their places, Neil watched to see who would be sitting where. Margaret would be at the head of the table of course, at the kitchen end. Sasha and Julie were already together on one side, leaving, he was pleased to see, two empty spaces on the other side for Courtenay and him. Sasha and Julie smiled across at him before turning again to each other.

He was happy to see them totally wrapped up in each other. Maybe, in time, Julie would move in with them. With the dog and all, they might even be a family.

Margaret came in carrying an oval plate, the brown chicken ringed by roast potatoes. Courtenay followed, carefully bringing in the gravy boat.

When the others had been served with chicken, stuffing, and roast potatoes, and were helping themselves to vegetables, Courtenay leaned over to put down Neil's plate. Her long, soft hair swung forward with the scent of flowers.

Neil looked around at his family and friends and knew his disappearing days were over. In every way that mattered, he had come home.

Acknowledgements

My thanks go to all at Nimbus Publishing for their excellent work, especially to the senior editor, Whitney Moran, for her faith in the book and her expert help, and to Tom Ryan for his patient and perceptive editing. Special thanks go to Allison McLay for her guidance on sensitive issues. I am also grateful to my family: to Alistair for all the discerning and long-suffering listening; to David for sharing his knowledge of horse matters, and to Edward for his encouragement and help. I should also like to thank all my friends for their support: Mary Borsky and the members of her writing class for all the good cheer and invaluable feedback; Genevieve Hone for her psychological insight; and Owen Menendez for his input on teenage diction and thinking. I must also acknowledge the influence of Ivan Coyote whose memoir-writing course years ago turned me into a writer.

Alan Dean Photography

Sonia Tilson was born in Swansea, South Wales, and educated at Monmouth School for Girls and Swansea University. She married and immigrated to Canada in 1964 and has lived mostly in Ottawa, teaching English at up to university level. Her first book, *The Monkey Puzzle Tree*, was published by Biblioasis in 2013, and was nominated for the Metcalf-Rooke Award in 2012 and for the Ottawa Book Award in 2014.